SEEKER

THE BOOKS OF SAM

JP FRANKHAM

First published in 2011
by Hirst Books

This edition
Published in 2024 by
Matthew James Publishing
matthewjamespublishing.com

an imprint of
Andrews UK Limited
West Wing Studios
Unit 166, The Mall
Luton, LU1 2TL
andrewsuk.com

Text copyright © 2024 JP Frankham

The right of JP Frankham to be identified as the author of this work has been asserted in accordance with the Copyright, Designs and Patents Act 1988.

All rights reserved. No reproduction, copy or transmission of this publication may be made without express prior written permission. No paragraph of this publication may be reproduced, copied or transmitted except with express prior written permission or in accordance with the provisions of the Copyright Act 1956 (as amended). Any person who commits any unauthorised act in relation to this publication may be liable to criminal prosecution and civil claims for damage.

All characters appearing in this work are fictitious.
Any resemblance to real persons, living
or dead, is purely coincidental.

In Memory of
Diane Taylor
14th February 1947 – 7th January 2024

*Sometimes there is no difference between
a stepmother and a birth mother.*

'A man can surely do what he wills to do,
But cannot determine what he wills.'

Arthur Schopenhauer

Contents

Prologue vii

1. Introductions 1
2. The Every Day 19
3. Sister Blister 35
4. Unconditional 48
5. Mixed Signals 61
6. Every Contingency 68
7. The Big Goodbye 86
8. What Happened to Robin Turner 92
9. The Wrong Man 101
10. A Meeting with Three 111
11. The Fires of Hunger 123
12. All for the Mission 133
13. Hunted 144
14. Without a Will 152
15. Out of the Shayde 165
Epilogue 177

Sam looked up as the head rolled along the floor.

'We really must get better guards,' he said with a sigh.

'Trust me, they won't help.'

Sam smiled at the man who walked into the inner sanctum. To Sam's left was a window, looking out across the ruined city that had been, in another life, his home. And at the heart of the city, the Pyramid of Sekhmet. It had been made for his wife, who was, even now, out there bringing forth their children. It was the most well-protected place in the domain, but if anybody was going to breach its defences, it was fitting that it be the man before him.

It had been a while since they had laid eyes on each other, at least five years, and time had not been good on his old friend. He looked old and worn, his shoulder-length hair now greying, his beard full. But there was a radiance about him that was new.

Sam suspected he knew why.

'Must we do this now?' he asked.

The man brandished his sword. 'It is time.'

Sam stood and approached the man, his eyes narrowing. It was as he suspected. 'I know this sword. How did you come by it?'

'How do you think?'

The hilt of the sword was fashioned in pure gold, while the silver blade shone like the sun, the inscription on it plain. Sam's eyes widened in wonder. 'Then it truly is time, Melkira.'

'Still you call me that...' Melkira almost smiled.

'It's the name I always preferred.' Sam sighed as he stepped back, still tired from his recent transformation. 'You could have said no.'

'Like you did? I didn't have the choice.'

At this Sam smiled. 'Really? How quickly you forget. Nineteen years ago, I didn't have a choice either. My path was pre-determined, at least that's what people kept telling me. Do you remember?'

'I do. But you did choose, eventually. Once the door in your mind was opened...'

'And before that? When was it? 2002.'

'Twenty-eight years ago. Outside a small café on Newington Green...'

Prologue

He was tired. Not so much physically, but just in general. Tired of life. And after 280 years, who could blame him?

Frederick had returned to Newington Green in the hope that he would feel a connection, a sense of purpose again. After all, it was here that he had first discovered his purpose in 1788, but after walking around for hours he still felt nothing but tiredness.

Nearly 215 years he had spent looking, studying, trying to understand, to prepare the way for a prophecy that would reshape not only his world but the world of his people. And now, as he neared the small café, he wondered if it had all been worth it. Had he wasted the last 215 years of life on a single mission, one that had taken over every other thing? He could have spent all that time with Celeste, leading his people instead of constantly isolating himself, surfacing only every now and then when Celeste requested him. Surely that would have been a more....

He stumbled, suddenly overcome with a pressure in his head that threw his balance entirely off kilter. He bumped into a young man sitting at a table, almost knocking a box out of the young man's hand.

'So sorry,' he said.

The young man tried to help steady him. 'It's okay, man.'

Frederick gathered himself together, trying to clear his head and regain his balance. His eyes never left the young man; the brown hair, the deep brown eyes, the baffled, almost concerned, expression. He lifted his sunglasses and peered closer at the young man, who pulled back in surprise.

'Hey, mate, you sure you're okay?'

'Yes, yes,' Frederick mumbled, righting himself. 'Sorry, yes, I'm fine now. Just for a moment there you reminded me of... someone else.' He shook his head. 'Excuse me.'

He continued into the café, his ears now attuned to the conversation the young man was having on his mobile phone.

'Sorry, dude, some old guy almost collapsed into me. Anyway, rating *Minority Report*...'

'Right, well I do, but what's that got to do with Cruise? It was a good movie, but Cruise... Sorry handsome but can't be agreeing with you on that score. His wife on the other hand, she's a babe!'

'What? Nicole Kidman?'

The voice on the other end of the phone whistled in appreciation, and the young man laughed. 'You do know they split last year, right?'

Frederick sat at a table near the door and asked the waitress for a simple Americano. There was a discarded newspaper on the table, so he picked it up and pretended to read. Still listening in...

'So, when you back, Will?' the voice on the phone asked.

Will. Frederick smiled. It was a good name, presumably short for William. He would find out. Because the presence he'd felt when he neared that young man...

'Don't tell me, more drama with the teenager?'

Frederick silently berated himself; he had missed some important information from the young man.

'Wouldn't mind so much if Ren was a teenager already, at least then she'd have a reason for being such a stroppy bitch. Ah well, you know how it is man, wouldn't be my sister and mother if they weren't having some kind of drama. Of course, they're probably giving Eon a headache, so swings and round-a-bouts.'

'Yeah, always a plus. Anyway handsome, I'll let you go.'

'Right, okay, cool. See you on the flip side, yeah?'

Frederick looked over the edge of the newspaper, silently acknowledged the waitress putting his coffee on the table and watched as the young man put his phone away. He stood, put everything back in the carrier and went to move off, but stopped suddenly and looked back at the shop.

Frederick flicked his eyes down at the newspaper just for a moment, long enough for the young man to turn away again. This he did, and Frederick continued watching him.

Giving him enough time to get some distance from the coffee shop, Frederick stood, dropped the newspaper and walked over to the now vacant table. All that remained of the young man's presence was a can of Pepsi. And on the lip of the can...

He lifted it and not caring if anybody noticed, licked the small drop of blood that sat on the can near the ring-pull. No doubt the young man had accidentally cut his finger. Not enough to matter, probably enough to sting but certainly more than enough for Frederick.

'Willem Townsend,' he muttered and set off from the café. He had intended to follow the young man at a safe distance but now he had tasted the blood Frederick had everything he needed. With a little concentration, he could easily track Willem, no matter where he might have been.

Which was just as well. He'd felt it when he bumped into Willem, of that he was now sure. And with that knowledge, all his doubts washed away and his purpose renewed.

At last, Frederick thought, *just as the Ancient promised.*

Nine Years Later

1. Introductions

William Townsend (not his birth name, but he liked to pretend and tell people that his name was William, but in truth it was Willem and man he had many a *discussion* with his folks about that!) tugged his jacket about him, wondering just what had possessed him to go to the park in such cold weather. Not one of his best ideas. Curtis, his two-and-a-half-year-old nephew, didn't seem to mind. Despite the circumstances, he always enjoyed spending time with his nephew and was happy for any opportunity given him, even if it was a result of another of his sister's 'crises'.

He didn't know the specifics, and at that moment he didn't much care; he could probably guess them, and he'd be right. Jimmy Aspinall, his sister's boyfriend and, consequently, Curtis' dad.

Will shook his head and brushed the thoughts aside; when Ren finally turned up for her son he'd no doubt hear all the usual excuses and be impressed by none of them. Right now, all he cared was that Curtis was safely away from the latest crisis and the shit no doubt surrounding it. Even if that meant visiting Ravenscourt Park (in the cold), Will was happy to indulge Curtis.

It was one of those odd March days where, although the sun had clearly put its hat on, the wind had decided to come out and play too. It wasn't anything close to a gale force, merely a light breeze but it was bitingly cold which left people like Will in the odd position of having a thick jacket on while at the same time wearing sunglasses to protect his sensitive eyes from the painful light.

He had spent much time in Ravenscourt Park back when he was a kid, having been brought up in nearby Chiswick. Plenty of memories; welly throwing competitions, inflatables, summer fairs. All good times.

As Curtis climbed the steps of the slide once more, Will looked around the play area they were in and felt a wave of sadness. It had changed so much since he was a child; gone were the small paddling pool and sandpit, replaced by more vandalised swings and even more dead space. There was so little for the kids to actually do in the play area. The swings were mostly buggered, the slide had more grip than his shoes and the roundabout was a source of more sweat than actual fun. To get even the slightest bit of speed required the kind of strength that Geoff Capes would have been proud to possess.

Geoff Capes!

Will really was feeling his age. It was this place; he hadn't visited Ravenscourt Park in years and the nostalgia was intoxicating.

The rumble of the train passing by on its way to Stamford Brook dragged his attention to the arches behind the play area. It was funny how times changed the way you associated things; back when he used to frequent Ravenscourt Park the arches were just further play areas with see-saws and the like. Now though, as he stood there he couldn't help but envisage Ricky and Phil working on cars, despite the fact that Ravenscourt Park was nowhere near Walford.

Will shook his head and looked back over the play area. It was empty except for him and Curtis, but nonetheless he saw children and parents everywhere; Ghosts of times long gone. Laughing and joking, the swings looking brand new as dads pushed their kids, the older brothers gently spinning the younger siblings on the roundabout. It was 1981, the year of mothers dressed in the mass-marketed Azzedine Alaia knock-offs and children with tight shorts and bright dresses. The boys were running around the park playing at being Indiana Jones, while most of the girls were combing the manes of Applejack or whatever *My Little Pony* they were lucky enough to own. Will at five was less interested in Indiana Jones than he was in the other craze that was then sweeping across the UK in the shape of the Rubik's Cube.

He could see himself sitting there, on the edge of the paddling pool, his feet dipping in, showing his skill with the cube to the kid who was destined to become his life-long best friend, Jake Caulfield.

Will smiled at the memory. It was one of the best times he could recall from his childhood, for all the wrong reasons. Most people tended to recall a time of closeness with their families, where they felt safe in the presence of their parents but not Will. It was the best time because Jake had only been living next door for two weeks and although he could never have expressed it at the time, Will knew he'd found the one true friend that would always be there.

They were at the park with Jake's mother, who the five-year-old Will found endlessly fascinating. It wasn't her amazing beauty but rather her accent. She was American! It seemed an odd thing to be fascinated by, looking back in an age where the internet had made the world so small, but back in the early '80s having an American family living next door was akin to living next to Buckingham Palace; Americans were only really seen at the cinema and on TV. Having a family who sounded like Buck Rodgers and Wilma Deering on the same street was the most exciting thing young Will could have imagined. It didn't take Will long to make friends with Jake, especially seeing as Jake ended up in the same class at school. Barely two weeks on and Will was out at the park with his new American friend, the two of them were inseparable.

Will sighed. He knew exactly why he'd come to Ravenscourt Park now. Things with Charlie were heating up and now they were verging on actual relationship material. It was a new thing for Will; never had he felt this way about someone. Well, not *strictly* true...

The enormity of what was coming was not lost on Will and so when Curtis had been dumped on him he had unconsciously chosen to take his nephew to the place he'd been happiest as a kid, when things were equally as new but in a different way.

He was brought out of his thoughts by a clunk behind him and an eek of pain from Curtis. He looked over. The boy had bumped his head trying to walk under the slide.

Curtis looked up at his uncle, his face scrunched up. 'Bumped my two-head,' he cried.

Will smiled at that, remembering what Jolene had told him about that time Curtis had met Tim, her four-year-old nephew. They were talking about Tim's forehead, which had acquired a nice bruise, when Curtis pointed at his own and told them that he had a two-head. It made sense, in a child-like way; if you're four you have a forehead, and if you're two you have a two-head. And so it would remain, at least until he was three. Will smiled. How long could he keep that joke going...?

Kneeling down so he was closer to Curtis' level, Will asked in a firm voice, 'Why are you crying?'

Through sniffs Curtis replied, 'For no reason.'

Well, Will couldn't argue with that but it wasn't the answer he'd been expecting. 'If for no reason, why are you crying?'

'Because it's naughty,' Curtis tried again, his two-and-a-half-year-old mind coming up with another of the responses he'd been taught.

Will laughed. 'No, it's not naughty this time. You're just being silly. You don't need to cry just because you bumped your two-head. Do you understand?'

Curtis sniffed, his bottom lip trembling. 'Yes.'

'Good,' Will said knowing full well that Curtis didn't quite get it yet and took a tissue out of his pocket. 'Now let's wipe those tears away before they become stuck to your face. You don't want that, do you?' he asked, his tone now light and playful.

'No,' Curtis replied, the sniffing dissipating. 'I look silly then.'

'Of course you would. Come here, give your uncle a skwudge!' Tears wiped away, Curtis embraced Will and for a moment the two remained like that, the unconditional love of his nephew warming Will's heart.

A slight vibration in his pocket and the unmistakable emotive vocals of Adam Levine alerted Will to an incoming message and he immediately released Curtis. 'Go on, play,' he said as he retrieved his phone from his jacket. He flipped it open and read the message from Charlie but beyond the phone, the blurred Curtis remained where he was, looking up at his uncle. Will sighed and returned his focus to Curtis. 'Shall we get you some chocolate?'

'A trick?'

Will smiled and took Curtis' little hand in his. 'Yes, we'll get you a Twix. Come on.' Together they left the play area, Curtis smiling at the thought of the upcoming 'trick'.

Will didn't notice, his attention was on the text message. He smiled broadly, feeling the familiar samba within and quickened his pace.

*

By the time he'd got through the traffic, Curtis was fast asleep in the booster seat, after nattering away to himself during the slow journey from Ravenscourt to Fulham Broadway. Will didn't want to wake the kid, but alas, Curtis was one of those light sleepers and as soon as Will unbuckled the straps Curtis began to stir.

Acting quickly, he scooped Curtis up and held him so that Curtis could rest his head on Will's shoulder. With the addition of a few soothing sounds, Curtis was soon back to sleep and Will rushed inside his house as quickly as he could, careful to keep Curtis' face out of direct contact with the oncoming cold breeze.

His house was a pretty typical affair from the outside; one of the many converted Victorian houses situated on Barclay Road, just off Fulham Broadway, but the ramshackle look of the outside belied the luxury within. It was left to appear a little rundown externally on purpose by Will; a safeguard against potential burglars. Despite its rise to prominence due to the recent development of Chelsea Football Club and the Broadway shopping centre, this area of Fulham was still quite known for its high rate of crime and burglary played a not-so-small part in that. Will, thanks to his coffee shop business which with three shops now was turning into a profitable small chain, was living quite comfortably.

Once the front door was closed behind him, Will dumped Curtis' little rucksack on the carpeted floor and kicked off his shoes before jogging up the first flight of stairs to the spare room.

Certain that Curtis wouldn't stir for a while, Will left the door open a crack and bounded downstairs into the lounge where his laptop was still sitting on the glass coffee table before the Como sofa. He opened the laptop only to discover that the battery was dead and only then recalled he hadn't bothered removing the charger from the laptop backpack when he'd returned home the previous night. He scouted around the room for the backpack. It was nowhere in the lounge that he could see, but as his eyes scanned the room one last time before giving up he spotted the charger lead sitting on the bottom shelf on the shelving unit. He grabbed the lead and plugged it in.

While the laptop powered up, Will headed into the kitchen to prepare a mug of coffee, smiling to himself. Not many got to see his scar, but once the laptop was ready to go it was Skype time and he was almost certain Charlie would be seeing the scar today.

Before even putting the kettle on, he released the lock off the back door and opened the top window above the sink. It was a thing with him; he didn't like the back door being locked while he was home and awake as he hated not having fresh air running through the house. Of course, the concept of 'fresh' air was a bit of an oxymoron in London but better to have external air running throughout the house than the stale air that circulated in a closed environment. The plants played their part in oxygenating the house but there was no harm in offering a little help.

The kettle now on the boil, Will checked in the lounge to see how the laptop was doing. It was all ready to go, he simply had to await the connection of the net. He opened Skype in preparation, just as he heard the back door open.

He let out a groan of disappointment, hardly able to believe his luck. The one time he didn't want his sister to come back early...

'Hazelnut Macchiato for me,' said a male voice which still, after all these years, contained a trace of an American accent.

Will smiled ruefully. Getting rid of his sister would have been difficult enough but getting rid of Jake while Amy was at work...? In what he would have called a mini strop had Curtis done it, Will slammed the laptop shut.

'Mate, kettle's boiled.' There was the scrape of a stool being pulled across the lino and Will knew that Jake was plonking himself by the back door so that his smoke wouldn't waft into the house.

Will grumbled silently to himself and pulled out his phone. 'Get making it then,' he called out to the kitchen, satisfied by the loud sigh he received in response. He could just imagine Jake stubbing the cigarette on the wall in the backyard before returning to the kitchen.

'Some host you are.'

Will smiled despite himself and began texting Charlie. On the way out to the kitchen, he bumped into Jake who was coming to have a nose.

'Shit, guy,' Jake said rubbing his shoulder, 'you should watch where you're going.'

Will looked incredulously at his best mate. Like he could hurt that brickhouse of a body. It was his own fault though, since he'd been so intent on quickly stashing his phone away that he'd got it stuck on a piece of thread in his pocket. 'Shut up, you girl. Coffee done?'

Jake eyed Will in mock pain. 'I thought I'd go for a latte today actually. Coffee is so last year.'

'Whatever. Shift your ass.'

Jake turned and headed back into the kitchen. 'Commencing the shifting of the ass,' he said, mincing his way ahead. Will couldn't help but laugh; no one could do camp as well as Jake and it was always guaranteed to get a laugh out of him.

Finally, the phone found its way into his pocket snugly and the good humour dripped coldly away. A few days ago, he wouldn't have cared for shit if Jake had known about Charlie but now he was relieved that his mate hadn't queried the whole delay with the phone. He wasn't quite sure why that was, and he was still frowning over it when he entered the kitchen.

Jake was sitting on the stool by the open door, puffing away at a freshly lit fag, his coffee cup sitting on the breakfast bar behind him. Will's own mug was still sitting next to the kettle, the open milk bottle beside it.

'You could have put the milk away, fella. Wouldn't have hurt you.'

Jake flicked some ash into the backyard and glanced over at the milk. 'I could have handsome, but then you'd be left with black coffee.'

'Lazy sod,' Will said, spying his milk-less coffee. 'And you couldn't have put it in mine because why?'

Jake shrugged. 'Don't remember signing up as your slave.'

Will narrowed his eyes. 'Right, whatever,' he said, sharper than he meant to. Not wishing to pursue it anymore, he poured his own milk and then returned the bottle to the fridge. He took a deep sip of his coffee; enjoying the heat as it surged down his throat. The caffeine hit his taste buds and he immediately felt better.

'Want to talk about it?'

Will closed his eyes and slowly turned to Jake. 'Usual shit,' he said knowing full well what Jake would infer from that.

'What's that prick done now?' Jake asked, all humour gone.

Jimmy wasn't Jake's favourite person. In fact, Will considered, he couldn't imagine Jimmy being anybody's favourite person. Will always got a kick out of the way Jake's whole demeanour changed whenever Jimmy's name was mentioned. Although Jake didn't work out, he was naturally a big man, much like his dad had been, and working on a construction site helped to maintain his muscles better than any gym would have done. Whenever Jimmy was mentioned, it was as if some automatic signal was sent to Jake's cardio system and the muscles immediately tensed. The new shaved head was a bit of a departure from his usual look (he'd had it shaved for Amy, his girlfriend of two months) and only helped to complete an ensemble of threat and danger.

'Same old, up to his eyeballs in shit. Ren has dumped Curtis on me.'

Jake looked around. 'Where is the champ?'

'Napping. I tell you, man, this ain't gonna end well.'

'That's a sure thing,' Jake said, his voice little more than a rumble now. 'You honestly need to let me take the fucker out.'

Someone needed to give Jimmy a good slap, but Will suspected it would take a lot more than that to sort the man out. He'd been nothing but trouble for Ren.

'Something tells me Amy wouldn't approve of that.'

Jake shrugged. 'No, but she doesn't need to know.' He sipped his coffee. 'Like he's much of a dad to the champ anyway.'

'Well, we know this but Ren insists that Jimmy dotes on Curtis.' Will raised his hands, warding off the derision that was about to erupt from Jake's mouth. 'Yes, we know it's bullshit but you ever tried telling her that?'

'Have you?' Jake asked pointedly.

'Of course,' came the sharp reply.

'Sure you have. Like never.' Jake finished his coffee and walked it over to the sink. 'I love you mate, but I keep telling you, you need to grow a backbone. Bitching to me about it really isn't doing Lawrencia any good.'

'Fine, I'll shut up then.' Knowing how sulky that sounded and not really caring much, Will picked up his mug and walked out of the kitchen.

'Yeah, real mature, handsome,' he heard Jake mumble.

Will narrowed his eyes but didn't respond. Instead, he flopped down on his chair and threw his feet on the stool. By the time Jake entered the lounge, the TV was on. *In the Night Garden* – the digital box having been left on CBeebies when he'd taken Curtis out earlier – was preferable to the little tiff he was having with Jake. That it was a silly little tiff was not lost on Will but for reasons he didn't want to entertain, he was irritated by what Jake was saying.

They didn't fall out very often, but when they did it stung.

'Will, I wasn't saying you should shut up. That's like hundreds of miles out from my point.' Jake sat himself on the couch and waited for Will to turn the TV either off or down.

For a short while he refused to do so, instead he continued to watch as Makka Pakka went about the Night Garden washing everything he came across with his sponge. Jake cleared his throat, but still Will refused to budge.

'Okay, you just sit here sulking. I'm sure when Curtis wakes up, he'll give you a conversation worthy of your newfound maturity.'

Once Will heard the back door shut, he turned the TV off but remained sitting there, gazing at nothing. He really was in a funk. Normally when he felt like this the first person he'd turn to was Jake, but...

He sat up and reached into his pocket for his phone. He'd apologise to Jake for being a twat, and assuming he hadn't pissed him off too much, then within minutes he'd be back and the two of them could talk.

Will knew his funk had nothing to do with the whole Ren and Jimmy issue, as much as that ticked him off it was pretty much business as usual, and sure Jake had hit a sore point about Will's bitching but still that was not the issue. Jake and he shared pretty much everything, all the big stuff, and what was developing between him and Charlie was pretty damn big.

He needed Jake in on this.

Just as he flipped open the phone, it vibrated in his hand and a message alert appeared on the screen. It was Charlie. He opened the message and read:

hey, u still busy if not im online still

With the broadest smile he'd probably ever wear, Will reached for the table and dragged it towards his chair, all thoughts of Jake having evaporated.

*

'Hello, darling.'

Frederick looked up, momentarily confused by the woman who had dared to enter his private thinking space.

'Just been to the Residence,' she continued. 'Celeste told me you were in town.'

The Residence was an old factory which the Three had purchased in the industrial area of West Canvey back in 1953, shortly after the North Sea Flood which had cost the lives of fifty-eight Canvey residents.

Canvey Island was separated from most of South Essex by a network of creeks and was prone to flood from the intense tides coming in from the North Sea but its seven square miles were protected by fifteen miles of concrete sea walls built in the '80s, as well as flood sirens and an internal surface storm drainage system which pumped the excess water back into the Estuary surrounding the island. Since the defences had been installed, Canvey had only suffered minor flooding. Of course, the Three wanted to be near the area of prophecy but not too near the central hub of activity in Southend, so Canvey seemed ideal.

Other than the Residence, Celeste pretty much left the industrial side of Canvey alone, but she had her fingers in much of the properties and amenities to the east of the island where the residential areas were constructed, including a small holiday camp and many seafront restaurants. Frederick shouldn't have been too surprised really; Celeste was a woman of affluence and could never settle for being a minor player in any place she spent much of her time. She was the same in her native France, owning more properties and businesses than most people would believe, but then she had been around long enough to build up quite a résumé.

The Residence was not very far from the marshes and within walking distance of Canvey Wick nature reserve, a place Frederick often spent time talking the small hours away with Celeste. And now, it seemed, someone else had entered his own special place.

He didn't recognise the woman, dressed in her very modern clothes, including that strange, and to Frederick it seemed entirely pointless, piece of attire called a shrug. Barely a fraction of a cardigan that just covered the shoulders.

'Don't recognise me new body?'

'No, I...' Frederick smiled. 'Isobel,' he said, recognition now dawning. 'Well, it has been a while. What brings you here? I hear tell that Harry keeps you quite busy in London.'

'That he does,' Isobel said, her accent more London than ever. 'And it's Izzy now. Gotta keep things fresh, ain't I?'

'If you say so.'

'Well, we can't all be stuck in the past. Specially if we got a Domain to keep in check. Gotta blend in, don'tcha?'

Frederick sighed. 'Is this why you've invaded my space? To babble at me in that awful faux-*cockeney* accent?'

'Bit of a snit, ain't ya?' Despite Frederick's warning look, Isobel continued to smile and sat next to him. 'What's keeping you all moody now then? Not still obsessing about your *mission*.'

'It's not an obsession, it's—'

Isobel laughed. 'Sure it is. It always was, from the moment I met ya...'

Frederick hadn't thought about that in a while. Had almost forgotten her part in things... 'When was that?'

'1788, darling. I ain't forgotten...'

*

Isobel Shelley waited, as she promised she would, but it was getting dark and the rain had begun to fall. She lifted her lantern, which she didn't really need, of course but appearances were important, and looked out to the northern carriage way. The Green was quiet, most people safely indoors, sheltered from the cold but Isobel could not be sure she wasn't being watched. The people who tended to gravitate to this place knew better than to take things for granted. Probably one of the many reasons she loved living on the Green.

The sound of hoof beats crunching gravel drifted over to her and she focused on the approaching shape. A gig pulled by a single horse, two people jostling about in the carriage as the wooden wheels managed to find every ditch and trough in the path. Both figures were dressed in the finest cloth; one looking down, his head bobbling about as if he were asleep but the second, holding the reins in his hands, was looking firmly ahead, mindful of the mood of the horse. The gig slowed and stopped right next to Isobel. She smiled, finally able to see the countenance of the young driver.

Young and as radiant as ever, Hareton Wesley smiled down at Isobel and tipped his bicorn hat. 'Miss Shelley, you are still a diamond of the first water, I see. A pleasure indeed.'

Isobel curtsied slightly, with a smile of her own. It had been some time since she had seen anything of Hareton and was not displeased to see him once more. 'Young Master Wesley, an' you and the gentleman like to follow me?'

The gentleman in question looked up, clearly not asleep. An austere-looking man of some fifty years (which certainly meant he was older), he raised an eyebrow at Isobel and edged his lip in the form of a very slight smile, which looked somewhat strange on such a Friday-faced man. Hareton looked at him, no doubt awaiting instruction, and the gentleman nodded. 'As Miss Shelley says, so shall it be,' the gentleman said in an accent that sounded almost German, although it had a cadence that Isobel could not quite place. She was not particularly well travelled but accents did not usually stump her so. 'Do lead on, dear lady.'

'As you wish,' Isobel said as she turned away, lantern still held aloft, and led the way across the Green.

*

Once the door was bolted, and the candles lit, all pretence of formality ceased. Isobel flung herself into Hareton's arms, and their lips met with great passion. For a full minute, they remained like that; any thought of the gentleman momentarily gone. Only the distant sound of movement in the room served to remind them that they were not alone. Eventually, a sharp clearing of the throat tore them apart and Isobel looked over at the gentleman demurely.

'Sorry. Hareton and I...'

'Have a history?' the gentleman asked, his face no longer as severe as it had been out in the rain. Indeed, his features now seemed to be full of warmth. He pulled up a seat and sat at the table, removing his hat and wig; both of which had become sodden in the rain. His hair beneath the wig was silver-grey, pulled back and clubbed with a black ribbon, his upper lip covered in an equally grey moustache, but it was his eyes that pulled Isobel in: deep brown mortal eyes, containing such compassion. It was rare to meet one of their kind with human eyes. Although they still managed to pass off as normal among the common folk, her eyes were pale, the pigment of the iris slowly fading with the passing of each year. And such was true of most of their people, except those who had yet to experience the Second Death. The gentleman before her was clearly one such person.

Isobel batted her eyelids bashfully like a betty, although she was anything but. However, it was an image she had maintained for a long time, fooling the gentry all through the Town, and she saw no reason to reveal her true self to a man she did not know. Even if he had been sent by the Three. 'Yes, sir, history we have.'

The man nodded and turned his eyes to Hareton. 'See to the horse, we shan't be here too long, I want them ready to go,' he said sharply.

Hareton bowed. 'Of course, Mr Holtzrichter.'

He turned to leave but was prevented by Isobel's hand on his shoulder. He glanced back at her and she looked at Mr Holtzrichter, steel in her pale eyes. Demure and prim might have been a role she liked to play with mortals around, but no one ordered another under her roof except her.

'You have both travelled far, and I will have neither of you leaving without full stomachs.' For a moment Isobel was certain Mr Holtzrichter was going to stand and strike her, such was the coldness that swept over his face, but it soon passed and he smiled, nodding sharply.

'Quite the chit, are you not?' he said, good humour in his voice.

'When the mood takes me, sir, but don't ever take it to mean I am bacon-brained,' Isobel returned, careful to keep her own tone light.

'Indeed not.'

Isobel returned his smile and curtsied, which brought laughter from Holtzrichter's belly. 'Very good, my dear, I like the cut of you.'

'Hareton, be seated,' Isobel said. 'I have a broth prepared already. Mr Holtzrichter and I can be alone shortly. To conduct our... business.'

Hareton walked over to the table and sat on one of the hard chairs, but he did not question the source of such business. Isobel felt sure he did not know, but he was not so foolish as to enquire in front of Mr Holtzrichter. Although he would return later. How could he not? He was on the high ropes and he, too, remembered their last encounter as clearly as she; it was an encounter both wished to repeat.

As she poured the broth into bowls for the two men she had to consider, once again, just why the Three would send a special envoy all the way from France to see her. Certainly, she had chosen her side during recent events, and she applauded the reforms the Lady Celeste had put into place over the last six months but she was one among tens of thousands of their kind in England and not worthy of such attention. It troubled her. Rumour had spread that Celeste was still removing her enemies, those who had taken sides with the Brotherhood. Could Celeste have been misinformed and now considered Isobel one such enemy?

She smiled at Mr Holtzrichter, who had offered his own smile upon receipt of his broth. Maybe she was looking too far into it, but there was something she didn't like hidden behind his smile. And his name... it sounded German, and didn't Celeste have a German consort?

Once the men had finished their broth, Hareton left to tend to the horse. Isobel busied herself with cleaning the bowls, all the while feeling Mr Holtzrichter's eyes on her back.

She stopped for a moment and asked; 'Is your name German?'

Mr Holtzrichter chuckled. 'No,' he said, 'although a common mistake. It is Prussian. I was born in a little town called Posen in 1722.'

Isobel turned to him. 'You are a young one, too, then,' she said with a coy smile. 'So you come from the home of the Tree King?'

For a moment Mr Holtzrichter looked confused, then he smiled. 'Oh yes, your mad King George,' he said, referring to the tale of the ailing king who had once shook the branch of a tree believing it to be King Frederick William, the incumbent ruler of Prussia.

'Hardly my mad king, Mr Holtzrichter. I have lived a long time, seen this country at war many times over, ruled by many fools. Still,' she added wistfully, 'it is my home, although I am very much no longer of Great Britain.'

Holtzrichter nodded in acknowledgement of this, and Isobel smiled, thinking that another hundred years of life and he too would not consider himself of any one country. Their people transcended the loyalties of mortal living. He was still young, despite his outward appearance, and he had much to learn. One thing he did know, though, was how to show his host respect. Holtzrichter had not needed to offer up such intimate information; age and birthplace were rarely a secret shared among their people and Isobel took it as a mark of respect.

'For myself, I am, as of this month, 179 years, born in London to a modest family. And, as you can see,' she added, indicating their surroundings, 'little has changed. Although let it be never said of me that I'll be found punting up the River Trick. Financially or else.'

'Being in debt is never something to be encouraged.' Holtzrichter frowned. 'You have lived over a century and thought to make nothing of yourself? If I may make so bold, why?'

'You misunderstand me, sir,' Isobel said and sat at the table. 'I choose to be like this, a woman of little means. You cannot live for over a century by attracting attention to yourself. As I said, this country has been at war with one country or another for so long now, an' I were to be noticed...' She shook her head. 'This is why I came to Newington Green. It has a history of attracting the dissidents, the outsiders, those who do not conform to the Church and the Crown and those who wish to remain invisible.'

Holtzrichter nodded. 'I understand. I was born poor and lived a very modest life until a visiting French noblewoman noticed me. She changed my life and now she wishes to change yours.'

Isobel was taken aback, but she had no doubt as to whom he meant. For a long moment, Isobel remained as she was. Then she asked, softly, 'Why me? I keep myself to myself, I...'

'We both know this is not quite true, do we not, Isabella?'

For the second time in as many minutes, she did not know what to say. She was certain she had kept her tracks well hidden. Of course, she had been dragged into the revolution but as far as most knew it was with open reluctance. Very few knew the truth, knew what exactly Isabella Firth had done during that violent time, and only a select few knew the true identity of Isabella Firth. It appeared one such person had talked. Isobel let out a sigh of defeat. 'I do not seek attention and...'

'That is why Celeste has sent me to you.' Holtzrichter said her name with such a feeling of intimacy it surprised Isobel.

The Lady Celeste was said to not keep many close to her, but it seemed Holtzrichter was one of those. If he was not the Lady Celeste's consort who was he to speak so freely of her?

'She heard of your involvement, the great service you did in the name of the Three...'

'They did not even exist then,' Isobel pointed out.

'No, of course, not as a body but as an ideal embodied in Celeste. Her desire to bring our people out of superstition, away from the monster of myth, has always been with her. Ever since...' Here Holtzrichter paused and looked down.

Isobel watched him closely. He knew a lot more about the Lady Celeste than he was willing to share. The mystery deepened; who was he? Isobel knew better than to ask, it was clear she would not be told.

'Since the beginning,' he continued, 'and it is that ideal for which you fought. As a thank you, she wishes to offer you something. Something,' Holtzrichter looked around the small room, 'you have clearly denied yourself.'

'Then perhaps it is something I still do not care to have,' Isobel said, beginning to have an inkling of what was about to be offered. 'I prefer to be unknown, Mr Holtzrichter.'

'Then, my dear lady, why did you fight in Celeste's name?'

'Because...' Isobel stopped.

For the first time in many many years, she felt she needed to explain herself. Perhaps it was because of what was about to be offered. She needed the Lady Celeste to understand why she stood against the Brotherhood and why she had to remain as she was. Working for the benefit of the Three in her own way. Isobel stood. 'Let me show you why. I shall return momentarily, sir.'

Isobel left her guest alone as she visited her private chambers where she slept and kept herself hidden from the world. She returned shortly, holding in her hands several sheets of parchment. She placed them before Holtzrichter, who watched her with great interest.

He spread the parchment out before him. 'And what are these?'

'A few years ago I was visited by one of our people, Mr Holtzrichter, a coxcomb named Edward Lomax.' Isobel shuddered with the memory. 'Something ailed him, sir, ghosts and voices; one too many maggots in the brain I shouldn't wonder. But still, he talked with great intelligence. No less queer in the attic as King George he may have been, but Edward Lomax was a man of learning and he brought with him the Book of Origin.'

Holtzrichter looked up, his dark eyes full of suspicion. Only the youngest of their people did not know of the Book and it was clear that Holtzrichter was not among them. Somewhere in the world there lived a being called the Ancient, the oldest of their kind and it was said that he was there at the beginning, in Egypt. The Book was his, notes of dreams and visions, tales of their combined history, everything from how their people came to be to prophecies of the future. The Book, it was said, was lost to the Ancient centuries ago and he scoured the world looking for it.

The look of disbelief in Holtzrichter's eyes no doubt matched hers four years ago when Edward Lomax had presented her with the Book.

She nodded. 'He was cast out of the Green after he murdered a family, leaving only the ten-year-old son without a tongue, but he took the Book with him. However, in his haste he left these behind.' Isobel pointed at the parchment. 'These pages, translated by Edward, tell of a prophecy about a man called Seker...'

'Seker?' Holtzrichter looked down at the pages. He reached into the breast pocket of his jacket and removed a quizzing glass. He picked up a piece of parchment and brought the glass close to it, not that he would need such a thing; their kind had perfect vision.

'Yes, believed to guard the gates of the underworld in Egypt mythology. These pages tell us that he will apparently return in the second millennium.' Isobel resumed her seat and found the relevant passage. '*And Seker shall return in fire, to bring the children back home to her.*'

Holtzrichter did not look up but continued reading. 'Do you mean that Julius was right?'

'I think he has diluted the truth. I do not fully understand what Julius teaches but I do know that what he claimed is a lie. According to the Book, we are at least over two hundred years away from Seker's arrival.'

Holtzrichter did not comment for a while, instead he read.

'This is why I followed Celeste,' Isobel continued. 'The Brotherhood sought to descend our people into chaos, and that is not the goal of Seker. We are not animals, despite our collective past, and we must prove that.'

Holtzrichter did not respond, instead his attention flickered from one piece of parchment to another. For a short while Isobel watched him, but it soon became obvious that he was no longer aware of her so she took her leave of him and slipped out to see Hareton.

*

'How could you have forgotten, my dear Freddy?' Isobel asked.

'It has been a long time.'

Isobel looked at him a moment, then laughed. 'Everything is a long time for us, but for you, this obsession has never left. You still live there, going over all your experiences, preparing for the Ancient's prophecy.' The more she spoke, Frederick noticed, the more her accent settled into something more authentic, like her true self being revealed.

'You, of all people, should know the importance. You believe in it as much as I.'

'Perhaps that was true once, but the world has turned so much since then.' She shook her head. 'I shall leave you to your thoughts,' she said, standing. 'And an apology. For bringing this to you in the first place.'

He looked up at her. 'Do not assume ownership of my actions.'

'Never. But I feel somewhat responsible.' She placed a hand on his shoulder and squeezed softly. 'Let it go, Frederick. We all need to move on.'

'For some, it is not so easy.'

For a moment she stared at him, her brows knotting. 'But why?'

Frederick could not tell her. Only one person knew... Well, two in a manner of speaking. And for now, that was enough.

'Keep watching, Isobel,' he said, 'and soon all will become clear.'

'Hmm.' Isobel pursed her lips. 'All right, darling,' she said, slipping back into her modern persona. 'I'll keep me peepers open. Catch you later.'

Frederick watched her go, his thoughts returning to that first encounter. He pulled his phone from his pocket and made a call to London.

2. The Every Day

Will glanced at his phone again, just in case, but there were no further messages so he placed it on the table and looked at the paperwork before him. Not that his mind was totally focusing on the job at hand.

Charlie was busy at work, which, in theory, gave Will a chance to catch up on some things that needed doing. He was, once again, in the office of the ever-troublesome shop on North End Road. He was beginning to get a little concerned with Kurt, the store manager, who seemed to have a knack for misplacing important paperwork, especially that which related to staff wages. Several complaints about being underpaid had reached his ears.

Before him, on the desk, was a hard copy of the rota for the last four weeks, amended to include sick days, overtime and so on. It was a point of procedure in Coffee @ Town's End that the rotas be planned a month in advance so that all the staff could organise their social lives accordingly. He could only imagine the havoc endlessly altered rotas would play with the lives of his staff and his theory was that if he kept his staff happy then he'd get the best out of them while at work. It was a theory proven time and time again, and he was proud to say that his shops probably had the lowest staff turnaround of any coffee shop in London; far lower than the big chains for sure.

The office computer was on. He sought to locate the file that told him who had been paid what on Friday. There should have been a hard copy of the document in the drawer alongside the staff rota for the last four weeks, but *nada*. So, Will had turned his attention to the computer wherein he ought to have been able to find the original file. He really didn't want to ask everyone to bring in their payslips because that would be a nuisance but he was seeing little choice since the staff wages records seemed to be nowhere on the system.

Unless... He needed some help, from the one person who understood the system better than he did. Stephen Krueger, the manager of the Kensington High Street shop. Will reached for the phone and pressed the quick dial button.

Within seconds the phone was answered and a young woman's voice said, 'Good morning, Coffee at Town's End, how can I help you?'

Will smiled to himself. 'Hi, is this Shannon?'

A momentary pause at the other end. 'Erm, yeah it is,' she replied, her professional voice forgotten for a moment. 'Who's this?'

'It's William. Is Stephen there?'

'He is, Mr Townsend,' Shannon said, switching to the consummate professional in a heartbeat. 'If you could just hold a moment, I'll get him.'

'Cheers,' Will said, always preferring to keep his dealings with the staff light.

It wasn't long before Steve picked up the line and said hello. His voice was unusually husky.

'All right, Steve, what's up? Not sounding your usual self there. Too much extreme sporting on the weekend with Robin?' he asked, mentioning the only person from Steve's private life that he knew of. He'd never met Robin but Will had heard Steve mention him a lot over the last eight years, usually concerning the high-risk sports that Steve seemed to enjoy so much.

'I wish. Nah, ain't seen Robin in a while.'

'Ah, so what's up?'

'Laryngitis, my doctor says.'

'Nasty.'

'Yeah, pretty much, but I'll deal. What...?' Steve stopped as a fit of coughing erupted over the phone. Will was glad they hadn't invented more interactive phones yet; otherwise, he expected his face would be covered in mucus by now. 'Sorry,' Steve said, his voice sounding even more strained. 'What can I do you for?'

The laryngitis was obviously getting to Steve more than he liked to admit since normally any phone call between them lasted a good ten minutes before they even thought to talk business. The banter was a key role in their relationship and it had always been so. Even now he could still remember the cocksure sixteen-year-old he had first employed back in '96 when he opened the very first coffee shop, not that Will had been much older at the time.

'Don't worry about it Steve, you sound awful. Why are you even at work? Surely Mandy can come in and run the shift?'

'She is. I'm in the office; audit day. Trying to rest my voice, drink lots of water – all that jazz. Doc says I only got Acute Laryngitis and it should pass in a few days.'

'Don't sound that cute to me, fella.'

This got Steve laughing; although by the sound of it, he wouldn't be thanking Will any time soon. Still, laughter was good for the soul, especially when ill. Even if it was an old joke.

'So, now you got me talking anyway, to what do I owe the honour?'

'There's been some kind of cock up with the wages and I'm trying to find the records on the computer, but *nada*!'

'Don't tell me, Kurt at North End, yeah?'

Will didn't answer; instead, he just waited for the inevitable comment.

'Told you he was shit. Worst mistake you ever made when you promoted him.'

Will agreed, *now*, but at the time he was convinced Kurt was right for the job. He knew the coffee shop business so well, but Kurt was a prime example that a good supervisor did not necessarily mean good manager material. Still, one bad business move in fifteen years wasn't a major issue. A bit of corrective coaching should solve the problem. Well, maybe more than a *bit*...

'Uh huh, you have pointed this out on occasion. *Anyway*, Kurt screwed up and now I can't find the records to check against the rotas. I'm assuming it's still on the computer system but you know me, never could get me head around this damn system. That's why I have a you.'

Will could just imagine Steve rolling his eyes, and yet at the same time falling for the bit of flattery.

'Okay, I'll come over and find the file for you. Anything to stick it to Kurt, but...'

'Yeah, go on, knew there'd be a but somewhere.'

'*But*,' Steve went on pointedly, 'you gotta come back here later and help me with this damn audit.'

As buts went, Will didn't mind that one. He was always up for crunching some figures. Still, one final little jab wouldn't hurt.

'And there was me thinking I was your boss.'

Will took a little pleasure in the painful laugh that spurted on the other end of the line as he ended the call.

*

'Cheers, doll,' Mike said to Marge, the big lady who worked at The Greasy Spoon (bit on the nose, but that was Marge in a nutshell) as she placed the plate of bacon and eggs on the table before him.

Marge didn't smile. Her grumpiness was almost patented. 'Only doll I've ever been is one of those Russian dolls,' she said, laughed sweetly, and returned to making more greasy food for the cafe customers.

Mike watched her go then turned to Jake. 'I don't get it; somehow I don't see Marge in a furry hat.'

Jake smacked him upside the head. 'I can see why you're a labourer, Mikey, you're as thick as pig shit. You must have seen those Russian dolls? Every time you open one there's a smaller one inside, until you get to one no bigger than your dick.'

Mike frowned at Jake's effrontery. 'Man, you're so funny. And this from the man who clearly has more East Asian blood than he likes to admit, if you know what I mean,' Mikey added, wriggling his little finger.

'Oh, I don't know,' Jake said with a wink. 'Amy hasn't complained yet. Reckons a small bump is kind of cute.'

'More comfortable when sitting down too,' Mikey said, adjusting his position as if to make his point.

The Greasy Spoon was their usual haunt for breakfast at the start of the week, making sure their bodies were full of cholesterol before returning to the building site. More often than not Mikey and he ended up working the whole week together but once in a while they found themselves at opposite ends of London and that was why their Monday morning binge of full English breakfast and several cups of tea was essential. Catch-up time for the weekend.

For Jake, though, there was a bigger reason than simply a mate's round-up. He loved Will, no doubt about it, and would do anything for him but when it came to being all laddish and talking about the things most guys talked about – the latest shag, football and generally acting like oafs for a bit – Will was just no good at those things. Jake didn't think it was totally due to his sexual orientation, a lot of it was simply just because of the person that Will was – low on fun and high on responsibility. Jake would have given anything to have Will along on one of the lads' nights out but Will and his lambic beers would be so out of place that it'd become embarrassing.

'How long before you move on then?' Mike asked. 'Two months has to be a record.'

Jake shrugged. 'Dunno, mate, things are going pretty well. See how long before I get bored.'

'Give you another week tops. I know you Jacob, me old mucker, and your little fella gets bored with dipping into the same pot for too long.' Mike stuffed his mouth with half a slice of toast and chewed. 'You know,' he said while spitting bits of toasted bread onto his plate, 'you could always try Will. There's a hole you've not explored.'

'Fuck off, man! I got nothing against Will being gay but he doesn't think of me that way. And, anyway, you're more his type.'

Mike baulked at this, but he couldn't deny it. When not in his scruffy work clothes and hardhat, Mike was something of a metrosexual; a pretty boy who preened himself in front of a mirror for a good hour before going out, every hair in perfect place and smelling like a tart's handbag. Judging from the few boyfriends Will had had over the years, Jake could easily see Will and Mikey together. Will liked them younger, too, and at twenty-eight Mike fitted the bill nicely.

'Don't know, mate,' Mike said. 'Wouldn't want to get between the unspoken thing you two have going on. You're pretty tight.'

'Well, d'uh, I've known him almost my whole life. And, you know, he doesn't really have the fun bags to hold on to.' Jake mimed groping a pair of breasts, an act that almost made Mike choke.

A cleared throat sounded behind them, and Jake turned around. Marge was giving him a look that told him to tone it down.

'Ah, come on, tell me your husband don't like playing with those bags?'

Marge shook her head and unconsciously nudged her rather ample breasts, instantly giving Jake a mental image of *Cissie & Ada*. 'You'll be lucky to find someone like me.'

Jake nodded in mock seriousness. 'True, so give me your number and I'll give you a call when I've tried out the rest of London.'

'Okay, hush it now stallion.'

Jake winked and turned back to Mike, who was shaking his head. 'What?'

'You'll try anyone once, won't you?'

'Sure, why not? All I ask is that she's female and free of disease.'

'Mate, you're gonna have to settle down one day,' Mike said, fingering his wedding ring.

Jake scoffed. 'Never going to happen, man, and if it does, it'll have to be with someone pretty special.'

'And that's not Amy?'

Jake knew Mike was ribbing him, but it was a loaded question. Two months was a long time for him, and their relationship was only getting better. Still, settling down...? Jake wasn't sure he'd ever be ready for that.

*

'Has it really been fourteen years?' Steve asked as he manoeuvred the mouse around the computer, opening file after file, locating backdoors.

Will was slightly envious, mindful of the countless times his own hand lost control of the mouse and accidentally closed documents without saving them, and here was Steve moving the cursor around like it was part of his own body.

'And almost five months. Yup, come September we'll be celebrating the fifteenth anniversary of the opening of the first Coffee at Town's End shop.'

'Can't believe I've known you that long.'

'And still, I know so little about you.'

'You know how it is, dude, social life and business not on my menus of mixers. Way it's always been.'

Will glanced down at his mobile which he was cradling in his hands; he was due a text off Charlie any moment. 'Ever since you were a spotty sixteen-year-old. You were crap with the ladies back then, too,' he added, repeating a very old joke.

'Look who's talking, matey.'

'I'm gay, what's your excuse?' Will raised his eyebrows and Steve let out a snort of derision. And then a throaty cough. Will chuckled. He'd lost count of how many times they'd been through that routine, although usually Steve wasn't ill. 'Be careful with that, I can't afford to catch it.'

'Laryngitis ain't contagious, fool,' Steve said, looking back at the monitor. 'Come on, baby, work for me. So, what, you off somewhere interesting?'

Will blinked, blindsided by the abrupt question. 'Huh?'

'Well, you don't want to get laryngitis so I'm assuming you've got something planned that... Well, shall we say involves your throat? Now...' Steve paused, clicking the mouse once, and turned triumphantly to Will. 'Got it!'

On the screen an Excel document opened, displaying the pay information Will needed to sort out the mess Kurt had made. 'Brilliant. I owe you one.'

'I know, that's why you're coming back to Ken High Street with me. Also, for the record, you might want to seriously have a word with Kurt. Sure, I know I don't like him so you can read this as slightly biased but there is no way that document would have been so embedded in the hard drive unless it was intentionally put there.'

Will frowned. 'Not even accidently?'

'No chance. Looks to me like he thought he'd removed the file permanently, but alas, or fortunately for you, nothing is ever totally deleted off a hard drive. You just need to know where to look.'

'Okay, that's slightly worrying.'

Steve coughed and reached for the glass of water he'd brought up to the office with him. 'I'd say so.'

Will looked to the floor, his eyes following the pattern of the rug. Disappointment was a nice way to put how he felt. He trusted the people who worked for him and in over fourteen years of business he had never had any cause to discipline a single one of them. Now, that it should be one of his shop managers...

'Can you sit in on the meeting? Take notes. I want to make sure that there are no misunderstandings here.' He looked up from the rug and the expression on Steve's thin face was as serious as Will had ever seen.

'That I can do.'

'Cheers.'

'When's Kurt in next?'

'Tomorrow. Is tomorrow good for you?'

Steve gave this some thought. 'Okay, tomorrow is cool. But I'd suggest not ringing Kurt, rather just lay it on him tomorrow. If he's up to some big scam he might decide to leg it rather than face the music.'

Will hadn't considered this. Despite the big let down his mind was still on its default setting; trust your employees, think the best of them and they'll think the best of themselves. 'You really think he'd do that?'

The look in Steve's blue eyes was enough of a response for Will. 'Also, I'd suggest you let him bring a witness in, too. Need to do this by the book, just in case things get nasty.'

'Shit,' Will said, taking a deep breath. If things did indeed get nasty he saw all kinds of possibilities – police, courts – it could go on for a while. He just didn't understand why someone would do something like… He stopped himself. Like what? He didn't even know what Kurt had done yet. 'Can we send this file across to the Kensington office, then we can crunch these figures and your audit at the same time?'

'Yeah. It's called email. You know the one; you're the net junkie here.'

Will made a face at Steve. 'Well, yeah obviously we can email it across but I just thought…'

Steve fought to hold back a laugh. 'You're really off your game today. Something to do with the call you're expecting?'

'Call? What call?'

Steve pointed at the mobile still being cupped by Will. 'The one you keep looking at your phone expecting.' For a moment Will felt like a kid caught out doing something particularly naughty, but Steve unknowingly gave him the perfect getout. 'You waiting to hear about the new shop?'

Will smiled, hopefully in a convincing manner. 'Anytime now.'

It wasn't a straight-out lie, after all, he was waiting to hear from Network Rail who were going to tell him if he got the lease on the unit at King's Cross Station. Getting a unit in one of London's biggest train stations would be the crowning achievement at this point in his career since it tended to only be the big chains that got hold of those units. Select

Service Partners was the biggest competition, with their various brands taking up most of the train station units in the country – everything from Upper Crust to Marks & Spencer. But if he could get a Coffee @ Town's End in a station; the potential revenue and exposure would set him on the road to becoming a proper chain, to the point where he could eventually form big business partnerships. But, of course, that wasn't the call he was waiting on, not that he was actually waiting on a call per se...

'Gonna be big potatoes,' Steve said, echoing the thoughts rushing through Will's head. 'At this rate, you're gonna need an area manager.'

'Angling for a promotion?'

'You know it makes sense,' Steve pointed out with a smile, which didn't waver when he added, 'so who are you really waiting to hear from? You've got a glow about you, and it's not one I've ever seen you with before. Not even when you were with that... Thingy? Oh, what was his name?'

Will swallowed hard. 'How'd you mean?'

Steve raised an eyebrow. 'What's his name? This new bloke, I mean.'

'Charlie.' The name popped out suddenly, and it left Will with a sense of relief. It was as if he'd been holding his breath for weeks and was only now able to breathe again. He grinned, no longer wanting to keep the news to himself. 'Email that document across and then I'll fill you in on the way to High Street Ken.'

*

'You're not freaking out on me,' Will pointed out, unsure whether to be disappointed or not.

There hadn't been much to tell, really, and it barely covered the five-minute journey up North End Road to the Talgarth Road junction. He was stuck in Steve's little '02 VW Lupo, his legs struggling to fit beneath the dashboard. It wasn't that Will was tall especially, but the passenger seat had got jammed one day after it had been moved forward to make space for one of Steve's larger friends.

'Why should I? Way I see it is that it's no different to being pen-pals, and many a romance has started out with two people being pen-pals,' Steve said and hissed his frustration at the still-red traffic lights. 'I swear they stay red here longer than anywhere else in London.'

Steve had a point about the pen-pals thing, and it was quite an enlightened view Will decided. Not a view he suspected many others would hold to.

'They only stay red to piss you off,' Will said. 'Either that or they're just helping you put off the audit.'

'Good thinking there, Sherlock.' Steve leaned forward and placed his palms together, looking up at the lights in mock-piety. 'Stay red, stay red.'

Will winced as the sun moved directly in front of his line of sight. He reached up and pulled the sun visor down.

'Eyes giving you jip?' Steve asked.

'Yeah. Been playing up all week. Well, more than usual anyway.'

'Forget your sunglasses?'

Will gave Steve a 'what do you think?' look, and Steve laughed.

'Well, that was pretty daft of you.'

'Daft pretty much sums up my entire mindset lately I think.'

'Nah. Nothing wrong with finding someone online. Isn't that the whole point of those chat room things? To hook up with people, make a connection? After all, for people like you, there has to be some way to meet new people in some meaningful way.'

Will wasn't too sure he liked the 'people like you' remark, but he conceded the point on account of the fact that Steve was actually making him feel better and less guilty. Although he still wasn't sure what there was to feel guilty about, nonetheless that unmistakable feeling was very much present. 'It doesn't help that chat rooms are mostly filled by weird people who are out to get laid, who have the social graces of pigs and can't spell for toffee. Which is actually kind of depressing in and of itself.'

'Really? See, I don't get that, you'd think with all this written communication peoples' spelling would improve not get worse. God, is that shop still there?'

'Huh?' Not for the first time Will was caught off guard by Steve's habit of segueing from one thing to another.

He was looking across the junction where North End Road continued on its way to Kensington High Street, at a small convenience store.

'Touch of Class; they've been there forever I'm sure. Remember them being there when I was in school.'

'Wasn't that long ago.'

'Wonder if the Khans still run the place?'

'Want to pop in and find out?'

Steve looked at Will like he was some mentally deficient child. 'Like they'd remember me? Anyway, green is go!'

And so it was. Steve released the handbrake, and the car went on its way.

Will didn't like the Lupo, it was what he liked to call a lazy car. He preferred to be in complete control when he was driving, and the point of an automatic was lost on him.

'Charlie wants me to go to Southend to spend a few days with him,' he said suddenly.

It was one of those things he wanted to lay on the table between him and Jake, but he was having the hardest time even broaching the subject of Charlie with Jake. Talking to Steve was so much easier for some reason. A notion that Will would never have thought possible.

'Cool,' Steve said just as quickly. 'You going to go?'

Good question. Will wanted to, that much was certain, but how could he just up and leave everything? His job, his family, his sister... The idea of being away for a few days and not being on hand to help out with Curtis did not sit well with him at all, and then there was Jake. In almost thirty years they'd barely been apart, saw each other almost every day. 'Don't know. Should I?'

'Dude, if you need to ask that question then damn right you do. I don't think you've ever taken a holiday in all the time I've known you. Bet you never had a day off school either did you?'

Will opened his mouth to refute that but found he couldn't. 'Well, no, I didn't. Someone had to achieve something in my family, and it was pretty clear it wasn't going to be anybody else. The only thing my dad has achieved is a closeness with drink and God, and look at my mother and sister...'

'Even more reason to go. You put way too much on yourself Will, always have as far as I can see. You've got no social life to speak of, other than having a few people over now and again for wine and fun on the Wii, a family that uses you like a hole in the wall and you keep Jake hanging around like a sick puppy.'

Will narrowed his eyes and looked over at Steve. 'Since when did you get all insightful?'

'Since always. I've known you for a decade and a half, dude, and unlike me, you're an open book. Listen, you do what you want to do, but seriously, doing something unexpected will probably do you well. You think I'm this reliable and good at my job because my private life is full of boring shit? Nope, always out there doing things that people would never expect of a responsible manager-type.' Steve winked at Will in a conspiratorial way that sent a shiver of excitement up his spine. 'Go, man, totally throw everything for a curve ball.'

Will wasn't too sure how to respond to that and was therefore quite relieved when his phone vibrated in his hand. He flipped it open and read the message from Charlie, asking him if he'd decided on whether he was coming or not.

Will looked at Steve who was apparently fully focused on driving up Kensington High Street, taking in the sights of all the shops and people as if they were brand new. Right, like he wasn't egging Will on in his silence.

Will grinned. Fuck it, Steve was right.

Need to arrange a time soon, he typed into his phone and hit the send button.

*

Izzy sat in the back of her car as her driver returned her to London. It had been fun spending some time at the Residence, hobnobbing with Celeste and Eryn. In her world, they were the closest thing to actual royalty and just spending time in their presence was something to be savoured. It didn't happen often.

Nonetheless, the time had been marred by the mood coming off Frederick in waves. He barely spoke, just kept himself to himself, constantly on the phone, sending messages and making calls. Izzy tried not to listen in, but at one point she was certain she heard the name Willem being mentioned. She didn't know who this Willem was, or indeed what the conversations were about, but they were clearly important.

Which meant, inevitably, it related to only one thing.

Frederick's obsession which she had introduced him to...

*

As she stepped out of the house and back into the rain, Isobel did up her pelisse, casting a look back at Mr Holtzrichter who still had his head in the pages. She closed the door and made her way to the stables, where she found Hareton readying the horse and gig for the long journey ahead of them. He looked up as soon as she entered, a smile stretching across his countenance. When she had last seen Hareton Wesley he had been only seventeen years, no longer a boy but not quite a man. Although, Isobel recalled with a flush, he had soon found his way around her body like a man used to a bit o' muslin. Now he was twenty-three, a young man, and she had to confess he had filled out quite well.

'Do you find me amiable?' he asked, enjoying the attention of her eyes.

'Very.' Isobel bolted the stable door and crossed over to him. 'You have become quite a man, Hareton,' she said, running a delicate hand across his firm jaw.

He held up a hand to stop her. 'What of Mr Holtzrichter?'

'He is else occupied, besides which I do not care a groat. Can he stop two people in the high ropes?' At this, Hareton lowered his hand and Isobel continued to stroke his jaw. 'I have heard word of your exploits these last six years, playing messenger to my people. And now to deliver the Lady Celeste's very own envoy?'

Hareton placed his hand over hers and brought it to his lips. 'Does this mean I have proven my loyalty?' he asked, kissing the tips of her fingers.

'It would appear so.'

'Then you will grant me my desire?'

'And what is it the young master desires?' Isobel asked, in her best meek voice, the tone of a doxy looking to please her master.

'To be with you forever,' he answered, gently pulling her towards him. As their bodies touched, he stepped backwards until he was resting against a wooden beam. 'In six years my desire has not wilted. Everything I have done has been for this moment.'

Isobel did not trust herself to speak. Six years ago, when the young Hareton had first come to Newington Green she had found herself compelled by his beauty but she could not give herself over to him, not in the way he wanted. A physical paring was one thing, but to give her heart to a mortal... it was bound to end in tears of blood. But that did not stop Hareton, even when he learned what she was. So she had sent him away; if he could prove his loyalty to her and her kind then she promised she would take him. That was six years ago when her world was not governed by rules. Now the Three were leading her people into a unified future of civilization and it was not for her to bring one into their ranks of her own accord.

But while he was here...

She pressed her body against Hareton's, feeling him harden beneath his breeches. He had indeed filled out, although not as much as she had hoped. Still, not one to be easily disappointed and knowing that greater length and girth was not the only way to pleasure, she whispered, 'Take me now, Hareton!'

As Hareton's hands undid the buttons that fastened her pelisse, Isobel lifted her face to the stable ceiling, allowing Hareton's tongue to play on her throat. His hands found their way inside her gown and reached to unlace the stays beneath, but his fingers barely found the lace when a banging came at the stable door. For a moment they looked at each other, Isobel's eyes daring Hareton to continue, but despite the desire burning in him Hareton removed his hands from Isobel's clothing and gently pushed her away.

Still a man of his age, Isobel realised with disdain, a man of scruple. She fastened her pelisse and watched him unbolt the door. If she truly took him, eventually, like every one of her people, he would soon realise he was no longer bound by the rules of the land.

Mr Holtzrichter stood outside the barn, the rain rinsing the powder from his hair down his face. He glanced at Hareton, who looked to the ground, his face flustered, and then at Isobel who merely smiled at him.

'I see,' he said with a curt nod. 'Miss Shelley, a moment of your time if you please.'

'Of course, sir,' she said, falling back into her public role, and stepped out of the stable. As she passed him, she noticed Holtzrichter give Hareton a lopsided grin of apology.

'Do beg the pardon of a gentleman for taking one so young off the high ropes.'

The younger man clearly did not know how to respond. So he stepped back further into the stable and turned back to the horse.

*

'It is good you have someone,' Holtzrichter said as he closed the door behind him. Isobel stopped by the table, waiting for him to elaborate. 'Later,' Holtzrichter said, with a wave of a hand. 'We shall return to that in a moment, but first these.' He indicated the parchment. 'I would like to take them to Lyon and study them further, if you have no further need of them?'

Isobel shrugged. She recognised that glint in Holtzrichter's eyes and was reminded for a moment of the vacant look in Edward Lomax's own eyes. Obsession. She did not know why the parchment interested Holtzrichter so, nor did she really care. 'If you so wish. Now, may we return to the reason for your visit?'

'Of course, dear lady,' Holtzrichter said, tucking the parchment into one of his Hessian boots. 'As you know our people have lived in disarray, with no rules or—'

'I do know, so if you would care to...?'

'Of course.' Holtzrichter smiled, and it was one borne of both surprise and respect. 'Celeste fears that war is coming soon to the human world, a war at the heart of which France will reside. Over the centuries our people have spent too much time involving themselves in such things and if we're to move ahead into civilisation then we *cannot* allow such distractions any more. It was such involvement that allowed the Brotherhood to get the foothold they did.'

'How does the Lady Celeste propose to stop this from happening again? It is human nature to involve themselves in things that do not concern them. A trait our people have yet to grow out of.'

'Agreed, which is why they need strong leadership. People who will show them. Eventually, we shall become one with this world again, walk side by side with humans, unseen and unsuspected for what we are. But it will take time and effort, and strong leaders. The Three are creating the domains, sections of the world led by a council of Lords and Ladies with clear directives. Celeste would like you to become Lady Isobel, of the Great Britain Domain.'

Isobel just stared at Holtzrichter. 'Me? I have told you; I like to remain—'

'Unnoticed. Yes, but you also told me why you opposed the Brotherhood, that you believe in the ideals that the Three represent. If our people are to emerge from the shackles of myth and legend, then we need people like you to show them how.' Holtzrichter regarded her and pulled a small piece of rolled-up parchment from his jacket. He placed it on the table. 'An invitation to attend the first meeting of the Domain Council. If you choose to accept this position, then the Three look forward to your attendance.'

Holtzrichter stepped towards Isobel and took her hand, which he kissed gently. 'Now I take my leave of you, My Lady, and I thank you for your hospitality.' He turned to leave, then looked back. 'One further thing. If you choose to accept this new position, then you will need someone who can support you... in all ways. I believe Mr Wesley would be parti for you and I do not see the Three opposing such a thing. In fact, they would encourage it.'

With that Holtzrichter removed himself from Isobel's home, leaving her looking at the rolled-up parchment still sitting on the table.

*

And now, leaving Southend, Izzy smiled. She had taken the Three up on their offer and had since ruled and guided the Great Britain Domain. And not only that... Even back then, almost 223 years ago, Frederick had been right about one thing.

She picked up her mobile phone and hit quick dial.

'Harry,' she said, her face now alight with a smile as her centuries-long husband, Hareton, answered. 'You would not believe who I saw while at the Residence.'

'Oh, my dear Isabella, tell me it was not Frederick...'

Izzy chuckled. 'Why, how did you ever guess?'

'Well, my dear, because while you were away word has reached me about his current obsession.'

And Izzy just knew who that would be. The mysterious Willem...

3. Sister Blister

The insistent banging soon roused him from his sleep, the echo of a dream still befuddling his reasoning.

For a moment, Will wondered where he was; but with a growing feeling of disappointment, he realised he was no longer in the arms of his lover. This brief down feeling soon turned to annoyance when he opened his eyes and found himself lying on his couch, topless and with his jeans only half-buttoned. For a few moments more he didn't move. He just looked up at the high artexed ceiling, abstractly thinking that he really needed to sort it out; artex was so done, it looked lame and reminded him too much of old folks long gone.

It had been a nice dream. He'd met up with Charlie and enjoyed the most amazing time. They had gone to a show, followed by a lovely meal in a swanky restaurant and they had talked loads, kissed even more and ended up back in Charlie's bed, and...

Will scowled, feeling the hardness in his shorts pushing tight against jeans misaligned by an uncomfortable night of sleep on the couch.

Still, the banging continued.

With a groan he forced himself to a sitting position, wondering who the hell would be knocking at his door so early in the morning and so damn incessantly. One name popped straight into his head.

Lawrencia.

Only his sister would think her problems were so important that they couldn't wait until a godlier hour before trying to find some kind of resolution. And worse, that it was a resolution that only Will could help with. Like he actually gave a crap.

He stood, adjusted himself, now that he was able to finally do so, straightened his jeans and looked around for his belt. Both the belt and his top were on the chair, so he stumbled over to get them. His laptop was still open, although it had powered down at some point during the night. Will didn't remember actually ending the Skype chat with Charlie, so he could only assume that one of them had said goodbye. He hoped he hadn't fallen asleep on Charlie, because that would be tantamount to relationship suicide, especially this early in. He certainly didn't think he'd done so, and the crunched cans lying beside the laptop gave him good reason as to why he failed to recall the closing moments.

He grinned as he did his buttons up and fed the belt through the hooks of his jeans; the conversation had certainly heated up last night, that much he did remember, but by that point he had been on his fourth can and after that... Well, he had no idea. He had never been a big drinker; the odd glass of wine when he settled down to a DVD, maybe a can or two when he was entertaining.

And now he had a headache to confirm his status as a lightweight drinker. The knocking on the door didn't help.

'Yeah, yeah, I'm coming, dammit,' he mumbled to himself and clipped the buckle of his belt. He picked up his top.

The blast of cold air as he opened the front door caught him full on his naked chest. He stepped back abruptly, almost closing the door on his sister's face accidentally. She glared at him but continued in regardless.

'Morning to you, too,' said her retreating form. 'Looks like you could do with a brew.'

Will remained by the still-open door and blinked. She wasn't wrong; coffee was definitely needed. Only black this time. He had an important meeting later in the day and attending in a hungover state was not a good idea. He shivered as the cold air hit him once again and closed the door.

'Mum's right, you're not eating properly, are you?' Ren asked as Will entered the kitchen.

He looked down at his naked torso. Okay, so he was quite thin but he was hardly malnourished or anything. And besides, his muscles, although never going to win him any competitions, looked quite sexy. Charlie said so.

'Right, and suddenly mother's grown a conscience?' he asked, pulling his top over his head.

Ren looked away at the question, choosing to focus her attention on the making of coffee. But before she did, Will noticed the haughty rolling of the eyes. It wasn't just the standard 'whatever you say' eye-rolling, it was full-on 'get over yourself' rolling. Very few people had mastered that little piece of body language as successfully as his mother, but in that moment Ren had it and for a split-second Will saw his mother as a twenty-one-year-old woman. Ren may have had her father's dark skin but she had inherited everything else of their mother.

'You and mum really need to sort this shit out, Billy, it's not good for either of you.'

'Yeah, can't see it happening any time soon.'

'When are you going to forgive her?' Ren asked over the crashing sound of the water from the tap.

'I don't know,' Will said coolly. 'When are you going to stop taking advantage of her guilt?'

The conversation died there, while Ren finished making the coffees. Will didn't want to start his day like this, already he was irritable about being woken up so sharply, and having Ren lecturing him was too much. If she continued he knew that it would lead to a few choice words from him about the whole Jimmy fiasco, and he could not be arsed with it at the moment. So, instead, he allowed the frosty air to melt a little and grabbed the milk from the fridge. He told her he was having it black this morning, and there followed a short exchange about late nights and the best hangover cures each knew. Spookily his little sister seemed to know more about hangovers than he did, but then he reckoned the best part of five years with Jimmy was enough cause to warrant more hangovers than his own life did.

'Where's Curtis?' he asked, cringing at the sharp bite of the coffee on his taste buds.

'At Mum's. Me and Jimmy have to go up to Manchester; he's got some business to sort out.' Ren at least had the decency to look away as she said that, which cushioned the blow a little. Will knew exactly what kind of business Jimmy was engaged in, and there was never anything even remotely legitimate about it. 'Thing is, Mum can only have Curtis for the day, she's off to bingo tonight, so I was going to ask if you could keep him here for the night?'

'I do have work early tomorrow,' Will pointed out, knowing full well he wasn't going to say no, but curious to see what kind of excuse his sister was going to ply him with today.

'I should be back by then.'

Will was surprised. No excuse translated into him taking Curtis to their mother's before work, since there was no way in hell Ren would be back early. He didn't doubt that she believed her reason for going with Jimmy was simply to make sure the twat didn't do anything too bad, but Will also knew that once there, in the company of Jimmy's mates, Ren's own judgment would wane and she'd soon be doped up like the rest of them.

As much as he hated the whole situation, he was glad she had enough sense to not take Curtis into it, too.

'Okay, fine. Tell Mother I'll pop over to pick him up at about six. Probably won't be able to get out of work any earlier than that since I'm likely going to end up on shift, depending on how things go with Kurt.'

Ren looked up from her coffee, and Will immediately knew she was not going to enquire about his problems at work. When she was a kid Ren had always been interested in what her big brother did, but then came the big blowout with her parents and the absconding to Manchester and Jimmy. He still hadn't got to the bottom of what had happened in those three years away, but since she'd been back her interest in the life of Will was relegated to how much she could get out of him, and using his place as a dumping ground for Curtis whenever the kid became an inconvenience.

'Can't you tell her? We're leaving as soon as I...'

Will looked down the hallway to the front door, all good feeling for his sister melting away. 'He's out there, ain't he?'

'Yeah.'

Will took a deep breath, itching to go outside and do some violence. Jimmy and he didn't often come into contact, and as far as Will was concerned it was probably for the best. He'd tried to help Jimmy a lot when he'd first come onto the scene, but all Jimmy had done was take Will for a ride and threw it all back in his face. There was no love lost between the two of them.

'So, how much then?'

Ren was caught off guard, and Will felt a glow of satisfaction, thinking that Steve would have been proud of his segue then.

'Money. You could have texted all this across while you were half way to Manchester, so you obviously knocked me up this early because you're after cash. So how much?'

'Erm,' Ren said, engaging her puppy dog look, but it was such an old trick that Will wondered how long before she realised it didn't actually work on him anymore. 'Well, we need petrol to get up to Manchester, and will probably need to stop off on the way for some food, and...'

Whatever Ren said after that Will didn't hear. He honestly didn't care; all he felt was disgust. Bad enough that he was woken so damn early, but that he was now essentially paying Jimmy to go and do some illegal deal up in Manchester... His mind couldn't really bear to hear any more of Ren's shit.

So he just walked back into the lounge and got his wallet off the mantle. Ren followed him into the room, and he handed her a couple of fifties.

She smiled at him. 'Thanks, Billy, we'll sort you out as soon as we get back.'

Will just grunted, not trusting himself to speak.

'Okay, got to go, see you tomorrow.' Ren pecked him on the cheek and left the room. Before she disappeared out of sight she glanced over at Will, and the look in her eyes said it all.

She knew she was fucking up again, but she felt trapped and could see no way out. Will would almost have called the look pleading, and although he knew he really ought to call her on it, he just turned away and stared at his reflection in the mirror hanging above the mantle.

The sound of the front door closing came a few seconds later, once Ren realised she wasn't going to get any other kind of help from her brother, and was shortly followed by the revving of whatever vehicle Jimmy had jacked to get them to Manchester.

'Weak-assed cock-sucking bitch,' Will hissed at the mirror. And it seemed as if, for a second, his reflection glared back at him accusingly.

*

The call last night had been productive, Frederick decided. Steps were in place, things moving ever closer... Soon he would have Willem just where he wanted him, and then... Prophecy would be fulfilled.

And it had been so long. Almost 220 years now, ever since his Second Death. He knew some thought of it as an obsession, but that was because they did not understand. Prophecy was not something that could be rushed or forced, you had to allow it to play out.

'I worry about you, *mon toujours*,' Celeste said from the doorway behind him.

He turned to face her. Dressed in a pleated white dress, her brown skin shone in the daylight that was cast through the high window. She moved towards him, seeming to glide across the floor, her grace unmatched even after all this time.

'You do not need to,' he told her. 'The time is almost at hand.'

'Are you sure?'

He nodded. 'Yes.'

'Then I believe you,' Celeste said, her voice solemn. 'We have waited in the Residence too long now, and I ache to return to Marseille.'

Frederick took her soft hands in his. 'I know. France is never far from your heart. It was always so...'

*

He looked up from the parchment, at the unwanted knock at his closed door. Things were getting ugly in France, another kind of revolution was underway, of the kind the Three had expressly forbidden their people to get involved in. Only two days ago the Civil Constitution of the Clergy was passed by the Assembly, despite King Louis' apparent objections. Even now Celeste was visiting the king to try and talk some sense into him. It always surprised Frederick, even after almost fifty-seven years, the way Celeste was able to talk her way into the confidence of those in power. He knew it should not surprise him, after all, Celeste was born of noble blood, and she was at home with nobility of every kind. Especially in her own country.

It frustrated him, too, that Celeste was becoming involved in the revolution sweeping France when it was she who created the Domain Council to prevent such involvement in worldly affairs. But there was no reasoning with her; France was her pet project, and she had to do her best to keep the forthcoming war she feared from the French borders. If Celeste were to be believed, there was nothing to be done; France would be at war within a few years. It was now inevitable.

He rose from the table, glancing one last time at the pile of parchment, and turned to the door. That also frustrated him. He had studied the words on the parchment many times in the last two years, ever since he had claimed them from Lady Isobel, and now he knew them word-perfect, but still he wanted to know more. In that time he had scoured all over and visited countless countries to uncover anything that would help him discover the answers he needed. So far all he had found were scraps; notes written in obscure languages that he could not read. Even the best translators found many of the languages difficult to understand. What he had read, though, intrigued him greatly, even if a lot of it was contradictory. Of one thing he was sure, he *had* to learn more, to find out the truth of where his people had come from. He had never believed the lies spread by the Brotherhood, but he was beginning to suspect that Julius, although undeniably egocentric and deranged, was closer to the truth than Frederick liked.

'What is it?' he demanded, as he flung the door open. Honoré, the head servant of Celeste's house, stood there, his face a mask of fear. 'Well, speak!'

'*Pardon, monsieur, un coursier a livré ce document pour vous,*' Honoré said and handed Frederick a rolled-up parchment, sealed with a red ribbon. Frederick's French was shaky at best, even though he'd been with a French woman for over fifty years, but he understood a few words. Someone had brought this document to the house for him. To take him from his studies it had better be of importance.

'Merci,' Frederick said, and turned from Honoré, unrolling the parchment. He stopped in his tracks and read the words written in the finely crafted script twice. He swallowed, span on his feet, and turned back to Honoré, who was already walking away from Frederick's room. 'Honoré, has Celeste returned?'

Honoré stopped and looked back, with a frown of concentration. '*Pardon, monsieur, je ne comprends pas.*'

Frederick growled. 'That is the problem, neither of us understand the...' He paused. 'Wait, I did understand that. Celeste, *elle est revenir?*' he asked, suddenly able to understand French.

Celeste always said that eventually he would be able to understand every language he heard, a peculiar trait that their people developed when near the Second Death. Which meant soon it would be time to... Frederick shook his head. No, he did not wish to contemplate what that meant. He knew, that was enough.

'She has, sir. I believe she is dining at this moment,' Honoré said.

'Thank you.'

Forgetting to close the door, Frederick swept past Honoré and made his way through the house to the dining room. There he found her sitting at the head of the table, resplendent in the finest silks, her dark red hair contrasting with the lighter shades of her dress. She looked up from her food, raised an eyebrow at Frederick's haste, and offered him an empty wine glass.

'*Mon toujours*, a pleasure as ever. What brings you here in such a hurry?'

Frederick sat himself at the table and took the glass, allowing Celeste to pour the red liquid out of the crystal decanter. He returned her smile and sipped before beginning. 'I have received a missive, an invitation from the Ancient himself.' Still hardly able to believe his eyes, Frederick handed the parchment over.

Celeste quietly read the script. Once finished she carefully placed it on the table and raised her pale eyes to look at Frederick. 'Moldavia. A long journey, Frederick, and a treacherous one. But such a summons cannot be ignored.' She smiled and reached a hand out to him, which he took and held in his. 'Perhaps you shall now have answers to these questions?'

'It would seem most probable. And, of course I shall go, how can I not? There have been reports of the Ancient for many years, but none have been substantiated in decades. Just rumour. And now Wamukota wishes to see... *me*? Why me? Why now?'

'You question too much, *mon toujours*, I have always said so. You always want to know things with certainty, to be sure and have no doubt. Such yearnings lead to a closed mind.'

Frederick shook his head. 'No, questions should be asked. Always.'

'Perhaps, but some answers are best left unknown.'

'Like the Second Death?' Frederick said softly, disturbed by the quake in his voice. 'It is coming soon, Celeste, I know it. I understood Honoré with perfect clarity.'

Celeste took this news with grace. She knew Honoré spoke only French, and she knew how difficult Frederick found learning their native tongue. She smiled sadly and placed a hand on his face. 'I will miss seeing these eyes, but you know what must be done.'

For a moment neither spoke another word.

Frederick swallowed. 'We shall see,' he said and bent down to kiss Celeste. She returned the kiss with passion. 'I shall return as soon as I am able. With answers,' he added.

Celeste raised her glass. 'To answers, may they be all you wish. And when you return, may you be as young and vibrant as when we met.'

Frederick bowed, then turned to leave. It was, as Celeste said, a long and treacherous journey ahead, through countries at war. Always, it seemed, humans were fighting over something. He shook his head. It did not matter. He would make it to Moldavia and meet with the Ancient, the oldest of their kind. And he would get the answers he sought. He just knew he would.

*

'And what answers they were,' Celeste now said. 'Answers and more questions.'

'Knowledge has to be sought, or it is not worth having.'

She smiled at Frederick. 'There are times when I think you are wisest among us.'

'Do not let Eryn hear you say that,' he returned with a slight laugh. 'She has always stood against me.'

'Pettiness that is unbecoming of the Three. But she keeps it in check.'

Frederick did not wish to contradict Celeste, but he knew she was wrong. Eryn had been against him since the beginning, and still, after two centuries, resented the fact that she only formed one third of the Three because Frederick had declined the position. His work on solving the mystery of their origins had consumed him from the moment he had first read the parchment, and months later, when the Three had been formed, he knew he could not give himself over to the service of their people in the way Celeste wanted.

'Perhaps,' Celeste said, 'once the Seeker has been revealed, you will rethink your position...?'

'And join the Three? That would be unfair on Eryn, and even if it were not...' Frederick shook his head. 'I cannot. Even with the Seeker revealed, there is so much to do.'

Celeste nodded sadly. 'So it will be then.' She turned to leave him to his ruminations, his planning, but stopped for a moment. 'How long until he is revealed?'

'Days,' Frederick said, his voice a whisper for fear of admitting it out loud. 'Days. I will bring him to us, as the Ancient promised.'

Her back still to him, Celeste nodded once more and left him alone.

*

'Good night, then?' Steve asked, trying to navigate his way across the now crowded office.

Will looked up from trying to re-arrange the seating; the small office really wasn't designed for any decent meetings. With one table, two chairs and a couple of filing cabinets, it was pretty much crowded. Trying to fit in two more chairs was proving quite a task. He managed to squeeze a third chair in so far, with a fourth still sitting in the hallway outside, waiting its turn to be compressed.

He was glad that Steve had agreed to attend the meeting. Truth was, if Steve had refused, as was his right, Will would have found someone else to stand in as a witness, but he preferred it to be Steve.

'It actually was,' Will said, in answer to Steve's question. 'What I remember of it.'

'Sweet,' Steve said, grinning like the proverbial feline from Cheshire. 'A few cans and a webcam, what could possibly go wrong?'

Will raised an eyebrow at that. For some reason he felt like he was back in school, coming in with stories of his first sexual conquest and being egged on by the most promiscuous in the class. Only he never did share stories of sexual conquests in school, mainly because he never had any. Knuckling down and getting the best grades was all he cared about back then. Now, he reflected, perhaps Jake had been right, he'd missed a big chunk of the whole teen bonding experience.

'Your laryngitis seems to have cleared up some,' he pointed out.

Steve shrugged and placed his glass of water on the table. 'Quick healer, mate. My body hasn't become dependent on drugs to get better.

Good immune system,' he said and coughed. 'Still, not completely gone,' he added with a grimace.

'So I see.'

Steve sat down and started leafing through the sheets of paper that were on the desk. 'What's next then?'

'Well,' Will began, giving up on even considering a fourth chair, 'I want you to take notes, make sure we get everything said down. Don't want to slip up on this. I'm still finding it hard to believe that Kurt would try to scam me like this. And yet the evidence...'

'...Pretty much says string the idiot up by the short and curlies,' Steve said, all trace of humour gone. 'And haven't you learned from last night that people often step out of character?'

Will thought back to last night on Skype, and nodded. Yep, that was definitely new for him. 'Maybe, but there are character types that people usually fall into, read about it on the net. Let me see; melancholy, sanguine... erm...'

Steve nodded slowly at this. 'Right,' he said, even slower. 'And we all know that the internet is a bastion of expert opinions. Only, you know, not. People are not like characters in a book, dude, you can't define them so easily, slotting them into particular personality types. People shift and change their attitudes, their desires, everything, all they need is the right... incentive.'

There was a distant smile on Steve's face as he said this, but Will wasn't sure he wanted to know the why of that. Instead, he kept his tone light.

'You really are the insightful professor of life, aren't you, Mr Krueger?'

'What can I say, Will, I'm multi-talented. And, you know, there's plenty going on in my world you'd not believe even if I did tell you. Not unless you experienced it yourself.'

Will narrowed his eyes. 'Is that an invite?'

'Don't know, mate, wouldn't be up to me. I'd have to ask Robin.'

'Right, the mysterious Robin Turner. Anyway, what did you say the other day about your mixer menu?'

'True that.' Steve nodded, lips pursed in thought. His face broke out into a wide grin. 'Maybe I'll have to speak to Robin. I know he wants to meet you.'

'You two talked about me?' That was a surprise. Probably shouldn't have been; after all, Steve spoke of Robin to Will.

A dark shadow passed across Steve's features, but an instant later it was gone. Will wondered what that was about, but he didn't get the chance to ask, as Steve leaned forward and asked, 'Anyhow, I meant what's next with you and Charlie?'

'Oh. Him.' Will waved a hand as if Charlie was the last thing on his mind. Steve was clearly not convinced by this attempt at indifference, so Will sat down in the chair he'd prepared for Kurt. 'Gonna meet up with him this weekend.'

'Ah.' Steve sat back and steepled his fingers, with a smile on his lips.

'Ah, what?'

'Nothing, just glad to see you're doing something about this. Been a long time.'

Will nodded. He couldn't argue with that. 'It has. Not since...' He shook his head. 'Wow. Jacen. Now there's a name I haven't really thought about in a long time.'

And it had been a long while, Will realised; a good three years in fact. Jacen and Will hadn't worked out too well, obviously since they were no longer dating, mostly because Jacen couldn't deal with Will's commitment to his work. Jacen wanted to go off and do stuff, experience the world a little, and he wouldn't have it when Will tried to explain they'd have plenty of time for that later when they were financially secure. Jacen had quickly found someone else; quite an adventurous guy from what Will had since heard.

'I wonder where he is now?'

'Probably off doing what you should have done a long time ago, Will,' Steve said, and let out a gentle cough.

'Still not too sure, though,' Will said, wondering what it was about Steve that made him want to open up so freely. 'I mean, Ren's fucked off again and I'm stuck with Curtis tonight. Not that I mind, since I love spending time with him, obviously, and better him being with me than around Jimmy, but what happens when I'm away? She can't just knock on my door whenever then.'

'So?' Steve held his hands up to ward off the words that were about to erupt from Will's mouth. 'Seriously, it's not your problem. You have your own life, and every once in a while you need to remember that.'

'That's a selfish attitude there, Steve.'

'Probably, but as Whoopi Goldberg once said, once in a while you need to give yourself permission to be selfish. You can't carry everyone all the time. Eventually, you'll buckle. And I hate to break this to you, Will, but you've been buckling for a while now.'

Will let out a breath of air. The truth coming from Steve was too much, and he wasn't entirely sure he wanted to hear it anymore. If this had been Jake then perhaps it would be different, since Jake had been there forever, but Steve, as much as Will liked him, was still the kid he'd hired back in '96. Hearing such personal observations was breaking a wall that Will didn't think ought to be broken. Yet at the same time he knew he couldn't talk to Jake about any of this; even now he could hear Jake's response, and Will wasn't ready to be slated by Jake for finding love.

Whoa. Will turned away from Steve, no longer able to take the inquisitive looks, and wondered where that had come from.

Love. That was a big admission, but was it actually true? Is that really what he was feeling?

The answers to such questions had to be put aside because at that moment there was a knock on the office door. Kurt had arrived.

4. Unconditional

Kurt couldn't give a good reason as to why the paperwork was missing and refused to admit that he deleted the original document, despite Steve going into extreme detail on how it was clearly removed on purpose. Will got lost on that technical stuff, but Steve knew his shit and it was clear from the look of anger in Kurt's eyes that he'd been found out. Ultimately Will decided to suspend Kurt on full pay while the matter was investigated further and pointed out that external investigators were being called in since he no longer felt he could deal with this impartially.

Kurt had stormed out, putting up a front of arrogance, claiming they could investigate all they wanted since he had nothing to hide. Although his colourful language indicated he knew he was screwed and could probably be done for theft and possibly fraud, since somewhere along the way wages had been lost and yet clearly paid out to someone.

A tense atmosphere was left in his wake, and although Steve attempted to lighten it with a few gags, Will just wanted out. But he knew that he couldn't go anywhere, since he had some paperwork to fill in before heading downstairs to run the shift. The only other person who could do so was at the hospital with her daughter, and so he was stuck on shift until half-five.

'Maybe you need to give Charlie a ding?' Steve suggested.

'Why?' Will said. Well, snapped. He knew he was snapping, but couldn't really help himself. 'I can deal with things without consulting my boyfriend.'

'Hmm.' Steve chewed his bottom lip, his raised-eyebrow look never wavering. 'Yes, I got that after years of seeing Mr Businessman here. But I was more thinking that perhaps you need to chill out a bit, and talking to your fella might do that for you.'

'You know what, Stephen, I don't need your advice. I'm the boss, you're the employee, let's keep it that way, yeah?'

'Sure,' Steve said and calmly stood. He gathered his things together, all the while making sure he didn't look at Will. Once he reached the door, he looked back. 'When you've worked out what's actually bothering you, you'll know where to find me. Later.'

Once the door was shut and Will was alone, he slammed his fist on the table. 'Fuck!'

For a while he sat there, looking at the closed door, his mind racing through all the things that were ticking him off. As usual, the business with his sister was up near the top; like a constant itch he couldn't reach, her situation bugged him. Kurt's own activities also kicked him in the teeth. Never before in his professional life had something seemed so personal to him. And now he was in an odd position with Steve. They'd always got on well, never been especially close, but the way he had snapped at Steve was totally out of order. The guy had helped him out with the Kurt problem, and had, apropos of nothing, helped him get his head around his relationship with Charlie. Maybe Steve had overstepped the bounds slightly with his advice on Will's personal life, but he couldn't deny that Steve was spot on.

He really was buckling.

Steve had also been right about the temporary fix. Later, when things had calmed down, Will would call Steve and apologise for being a jerk to him. But right now he had another call to make.

As he speed-dialled Charlie's number, he glanced up at the clock on the wall. Charlie was at work, but hopefully he was on a break.

'Hey, lover boy, you all right?'

Upon hearing Charlie's light voice Will decided that, yes, he was indeed all right. Now.

*

Frederick ended the call. It was almost amusing how easily some people were appeased, how just a few words could bring someone down. All credit to him, of course, since he had spent a lot of time cultivating the relationship, portraying himself as the calm island in a turbulent ocean.

'Soon,' he said to himself. 'Soon.'

He stepped out of the Residence into the fresh air of Canvey Island. He needed to take a trip to Leigh. He had a few old friends to see, plus an errand to run for Celeste.

He didn't mind. She had been so patient with him, and now things were drawing ever closer, he knew he owed her some of his time. In over two centuries she had asked so little of him, always let him get on with his studies, his travels, his search for answers.

'You ready then, are you?'

Frederick froze at the sound of the Welsh accent. He closed his eyes.

'Eryn,' he said, 'what the hell do you want?'

'Going with you, en't I?'

Frederick looked at her. 'I think I can talk to Rhys on my own.'

Eryn shrugged. 'Maybe, but Celeste decided it was best to have one of the Three there. Adds a little extra emphasis.'

Somehow Frederick doubted that was true. Over the last two centuries he had served as Envoy of the Three on many occasions; their people knew him well, knew that when he came calling officially he was speaking on behalf of the Three. Celeste knew this too. It seemed more likely Eryn had decided she wanted to tag along, to see if Frederick was up to something. No doubt she'd already sussed out that Frederick and Celeste were having private talks while they all stayed at the Residence and no doubt Eryn had some idea what those talks were about. And if there was one thing Eryn did not like, it was being kept out of the loop.

'Fine. Whatever. Just add emphasis then, and let me do the talking.'

Frederick moved on without any warning, causing Eryn to jog briefly to catch up.

'I don't know what's your problem,' she said to him. 'You've enjoyed a lot of autonomy over the years because *we* have allowed it. It doesn't make you special.'

Frederick glanced down at Eryn. 'Next time, get a bigger vessel. I think you've developed *small man syndrome*. Always feeling persecuted. It's not a good look.'

'Well, at least I chose my vessel with care. I didn't just jump a kid in the open, and worse, leave my old vessel behind to be found by the police. Sloppy and careless.'

'Was it? Or was it intentional...?'

'So, you intentionally wanted to draw attention? We have survived for two hundred years by not being seen. By being a part of the world, but not of it. By controlling things, guiding things, we—'

'Spare me the dogma, Iestyn!'

It was a low blow. Using what was, to all intents and purposes, a dead name now. Since 1987, since Eryn had decided to become a woman, Iestyn was dead. And it was understood among their people that if someone chose to switch genders, to get a new identity, they were not to speak of the old identity again. It was, at the very least, considered bad taste, at worst an unpardonable insult.

'You know, it's funny, for someone who has spent so long searching for the answers to our own history, how easily you flaunt and dismiss what we've been through over the centuries.' Eryn stopped, forcing Frederick to stop too. 'You disgust me,' she said, pouring every ounce of loathing into those words that she could.

Frederick remained there a moment, watching her carry on without him.

Sometimes I disgust myself, he thought. But then quickly dismissed the admonition. In the pursuit of truth, none of it mattered. The manufactured world of rules they all lived in; when he found the Seeker, when together they uncovered the truth of their origins, then people like Eryn would see.

The last couple of centuries of order would mean nothing.

*

The short chat with Charlie did the trick, leaving Will in an effervescent mood that carried him nicely through the following shift. He quite enjoyed the actual work, interacting with the customers. It had been a while since he'd done some proper hands-on work at his shops, so it was nice to just chat and talk about coffee instead of looking at figures and planning for a new shop in a busy train station.

Of course, being the big boss did come with a few cons, in particular an edginess to the staff, who acted in a very stilted manner for the first hour or two, while he sought ways to convince them that he wasn't there to watch them and that they really should act as if he was just another of the guys. Eventually, the message did get through and he finally saw the real world according to the staff of Coffee @ Town's End. And he liked what he saw.

The staff were great at their jobs, always friendly and welcoming to the customers, but clownish in equal measure behind the scenes. It was a work ethic he wholly approved of; if work wasn't fun then there really was no point to it.

The good vibes stayed with him as he travelled to his mother's, and he refused to allow her husband to bring him down. He had already decided that he would invite Jake over for the evening; it had been a long time since they'd pulled an all-nighter and now was as good a time as any, plus it was time for him to tell Jake all about Charlie. And he had just the way into the conversation.

En route to his mother's, he tried calling Steve but the line was dead. Not put off, once he pulled up outside his mother's house, Will sent Steve a text apologising for his unforgivable snappiness earlier.

Picking up Curtis was relatively painless and formal. Barely a word was passed between Will and Eon; technically his step-dad, Will never thought of Eon as anything but his mother's husband. As ever the looks of ill-concealed disgust levelled at him went unnoticed by his mother. She kindly left him in the living room, while she went about getting Curtis' stuff together; the idea of actually having it all ready in time for Curtis to be picked up clearly did not occur to her. Instead, she'd rather spend her energies bitching about being dumped on by Lawrencia and how it played havoc with her night.

'You could have said no,' Will pointed out.

His mother rolled her eyes at that idea, and Will had to hide a smile. Yes, Ren was definitely her daughter. 'No, I couldn't, Billy, and you know why.'

'Right, just like you know I hate that name.'

At that, his mother ignored him. A symptom of a bigger problem in his family. The bloody-mindedness of the women, refusing to compromise or change their views on anything.

The whole reason Lawrencia had absconded to Manchester five years ago was because of a flaming row she'd had with their mother, who had forbidden her to do something or other, but it was just another example of two people so alike that all they could do was butt-heads. And ever since Ren had come back his mother had almost bent over backwards to accommodate her in fear that she might up and leave again at the first sign of resistance.

As his mother continued to busy herself, Will chose to wander up the stairs to where Curtis was playing. The boy didn't hear Will approach, so he stood at the doorway for a short while, as Curtis played with his little cars. Watching his nephew transported him back almost thirty years, and he saw himself in the very same room with Jake playing with Matchbox cars. Will had a bucket full of random cars, way more than any kid really needed, and was often getting in trouble for laying them out all the way down the stairs. Will smiled at the memory.

It was a happy home back then, just him and his parents, almost a decade before the big divorce came along after his mother's affair with Eon Adomako was discovered and his dad was kicked out of his own house.

Various other small events followed; key moments in Will's life marked by abrupt changes that sent his dad to the arms of Jesus and led to the birth of his sister in 1990, by which time Eon had already moved into the house and made it his home. Will had to suffer a few excruciating years before he was able to move into a student flat when he started college.

It was in moments like this, as he was dragged back to easier times, that he wondered how his life would have differed if he'd not gone to college. Would he be in Jake's place now? Going from job to job, coasting through life, but always having fun and rarely being left alone. Would he have stayed at home, been there for Lawrencia from her birth, and found a middle ground of understanding with the man who became his stepdad? He didn't know.

He'd read lots of literature on the more esoteric beliefs and sometimes thought his life would have turned out the way it did regardless of his choices as a teen. Events would have conspired against him to make him the man he was. But for that moment he lost himself in the thought that maybe, just maybe, it was not too late to change the man he had become.

'Undle Billy!'

Will snapped out of his private place and came crashing back to reality as a bundle of child ran into his legs. The only person he didn't mind calling him Billy – it was a child's name, not that of a responsible adult. So having a child use the name was okay. Will reached down and scooped Curtis up.

'Hey, buddy, how you doing?'

'I fine. Grampy buyed me new car.'

'Did he? Wow, which one?' Will asked, returning Curtis to the floor. The kid scrambled over to his pile of cars and picked out the shiny new one. 'That's brilliant! What car is it?'

'Blue one,' Curtis said, as if that was obvious. And indeed it was blue, but usually Curtis gave his cars names. Clearly, the shiny blue one didn't deserve a name, maybe because Grampy bought it, Will thought ruthlessly.

'Right, then, shall we put these away? You're coming to Uncle Billy's tonight.'

Curtis lowered his head. 'Mummy and Daddy left me,' he said quietly, his solemn voice reaching right in and pulling the biggest heartstring it could find.

Will swallowed hard and knelt down beside his nephew. 'I'm always here for you, buddy. Uncle Billy will never leave you.'

For a moment Curtis didn't look up, instead he continued to look at the car in his hand. Then he dropped the car, looked up and smiled the most rewarding smile Will had ever seen.

'Come here,' he said and took Curtis in his arms. 'I love you.'

'How much?' Curtis' muffled voice asked.

Will released Curtis and threw his arms as far apart as he was able. 'This much!'

'That big much. I love you this much in the whole world,' Curtis said, also throwing his chubby arms out wide.

Will grinned, wishing all love was so easy to find.

*

'Happy now?' Frederick asked as they stepped out of the small café.

'Are you?' Eryn asked.

Frederick would have been happier if Eryn had said nothing during the meeting with Rhys, but she couldn't help herself. She had to place her stamp on things, make sure Rhys knew she outranked Frederick and had much more of a say. Him alone would have been enough, but Frederick supposed having Eryn there, *emphasising* the Three's position, would be enough to keep Rhys in check. They all knew he'd been doing some dodgy dealing, and Frederick liked to believe there was a better way of handling that, a most subtle way, but Eryn's presence was at least quicker.

Without a word, he turned from Eryn.

'Where are you going?' she asked.

Frederick glanced back. 'What is it to you, Eryn? I have my own things to do. I mean, maybe you forgot, but I actually live in this town. I have a life.'

'Oh, the irony.' Eryn shook her head and waved Frederick on. 'Go on then, enjoy your borrowed life.'

Frederick stopped. 'Borrowed...? That's all we have, Eryn. Every single one of us. We haven't had our own lives since our Second Deaths. Unlike the Three, most of us do live in this world. Are a part of it. Like every single day.'

Eryn shrugged. 'If you say so.'

She turned and walked away, saying nothing more. And, for some reason, that incensed Frederick more than anything else she had said or done since leaving the Residence with him.

*

Nervous. Will didn't understand it. They'd known each other since they were five, and now after almost a life time of friendship he was nervous at the prospect of Jake arriving. It was patently absurd to the nth degree.

The evening thus far, despite the brief interlude at his mother's, had been enjoyable enough; spending time with Curtis for an hour before the kid was too tired to play anymore, he'd got a response from Steve who said things were cool and he hoped Will would have things sorted by the next time they caught each other, Will replied saying that after tonight things would indeed be sorted, one way or another, since Jake was coming over after he'd been to see Amy. That Jake was not arriving too soon was okay by Will, since it gave him time to get a call in to Charlie.

Will felt quite encouraged once the call had ended since Charlie agreed that telling Jake was a good thing. If nothing else it'd show Will once and for all where they all stood, although Will was absolutely convinced he knew how Jake would take the news. But Charlie wasn't as sure; in his mind, people often surprised you when you least expected it, and from what Will had told him about his relationship with Jake, Charlie was certain Will was going to be surprised. Will couldn't agree, since he knew Jake better and his mind was quite narrow about these things, and besides he read too many crazy stories in the papers about weirdoes on the net to be happy about this.

The call closed on Charlie wishing Will luck and getting him to promise to keep his mind open. Leave the preconceptions at the door, and see what happened. Will said he'd do his best.

And so there he was, sitting on his favourite chair, nerves playing havoc with his system, his eyes darting from the TV to the bay window at every blurred person who walked past. It was nuts, his mind was distracted. As his eyes continued to shift between TV and window, his mind ran through every possible scenario, and none of them ended well.

The vibration of his phone in his pocket scared the living shit out of him. He pulled it out, laughing at his own stupidity, to see it was a text message from Jake. He was ten minutes away, so the kettle needed to go on. For a moment Will stared at the empty screen, uncertain as to how he ought to respond. He didn't want Jake to suspect something was up, but by the same token, he didn't want to seem too casual either. Will settled for a 'rightio', and wandered into the kitchen.

The water boiled and he pulled two mugs out of the cupboard.

He stared at the mugs. His hands seemed so far away from his body, and for the life of him he had no idea what he was doing. He blinked, disturbed by the dissociation, and placed the mugs on the side. Dizziness followed the vertigo and he reached out to steady himself, whoever he was.

He looked up, alarmed by the lack of awareness he felt about himself. The kitchen was alien to him, everything around him was wrong, not even remotely familiar.

'I'm not ready,' he mumbled, as a distant memory threatened to crash in.

*

Just as he approached the pub, Frederick stumbled.

The world around him spun and in his mind... It felt like something was crashing in. An alien presence. Something he did not recognise. And a voice...

'I'm not ready.'

It was familiar. One he knew, but as the voice faded, so did the association.

For a moment longer, Frederick stood there. He righted himself, made sure the world had stopped spinning, and took a deep breath.

That was new.

And at that, he couldn't help but smile. He had lived for so long, and to experience something so truly new...? It was exhilarating.

He needed a drink. Not alcohol, though, a *real* drink. Of the sort they served in the private backroom of the pub.

*

The moment passed and for a bizarre second Will felt as if he'd just returned home from a very long journey. He shook his head, completely confused by the experience, and chanced a look at the clock on the wall.

He blinked the blurred vision away and stared closer. How could he have been in the kitchen for twenty minutes? He'd only just pulled the mugs out of the cupboard. The kettle was still... No, he realised, seeing no sign of steam, the kettle was not boiling at all. He placed a hand against the metal, surprised to find that it was only slightly warm.

He snapped his head around at the thump on the kitchen door. Jake was standing outside, his face pressed up against the frosted glass. Disjointedly, Will crossed the kitchen floor and unlocked the door, wondering when he'd locked it.

'You okay, handsome?' Jake asked once he was inside.

'I...' Will honestly didn't know. Nothing like this had ever happened to him before. 'Of course, I'm good, man. What's in the bag?' he asked, nodding at the carrier in Jake's hand.

Jake eyed Will, clearly not buying it, but Will held his look. Jake shrugged and looked down, reaching into the bag as he did so. With Jake's attention distracted, Will let out a quiet sigh of relief and turned back to the kettle.

'Tonight's entertainment,' Jake said, behind him, 'just in case we run out of things to do. Only one thing goes well with munch, other than deep and insightful conversation brought on by over-tiredness. Movies!'

Will turned from spooning the coffee into the mugs and looked at the DVDs Jake was holding. 'Don't you think I got enough DVDs of my own?'

'Well, yeah, sure you have, but we've seen them all to death. Figured it was about time we broadened that mind of yours.'

Nice turn of phrase there, Will thought. 'Broadening of the mind is good,' he said out loud, thinking that could be the slogan for the all-nighter ahead.

'What first then? *Waiting* or *Thor*?'

'*Thor*? That's not even hit the cinemas yet, how did you...?'

Jake smiled. 'Got my contacts, man.'

Will took the DVD off Jake. It was in a plastic slip-case, with a badly photocopied cover. 'Chris Hemsworth,' he said, smiling. 'Rocking the long hair.'

'Thought you'd like that. Although, from the set pictures I've seen, it looks like a poor man's *Flash Gordon*.'

Will agreed. 'They did well with the Iron Man and Hulk films, so...' He ran his fingers over the cover. 'But Hemsworth with long hair...' He pretended to weigh it up. 'Shit sets, but Hemsworth muscled up with long hair. I reckon I can live with it.'

Jake laughed and picked up his coffee. 'I bet.' After taking a sip he said, 'Ah, no one can make a coffee like you.'

'Hence why I own a chain of coffee shops, eh?' Will looked up from the DVD. 'Not that it matters, since clearly this one wins, but what's the other DVD?'

'Don't know a lot about this one. But Mike swears by it, says it's the funniest shit. By the same people who made *American Pie*; it's all about the people who work in a restaurant and the crazy shit they get up to. Like this thing called the brain. What you do is—'

'Well, *American Pie* was good, so I'll give you a point for that, but the sequels...'

'Were lame. Yeah, that's a given. This one has Ryan Reynolds in it, mind.'

Now Will was interested. 'Well, he's buff too...'

'And to think I thought you chose films on artistic merit.'

Will smirked at that. 'Sometimes, but a bit of totty doesn't hurt.'

'Fair. So, what'll it be?'

'See how the mood takes us later? You know us, once we get talking before we know it it'll be morning and we won't have even bothered with a DVD.'

Jake nodded. 'Won't be the first time.'

'And besides, you can always leave *Thor* here and I'll watch it another time.'

'I could,' Jake said, as he crossed the kitchen and peered into the food cupboard. 'So, you stocked up on munch? I seem to have a craving for... Ah! Just the thing!' He turned away from the cupboard brandishing a packet of Ritz Crackers. 'Wow, they still make these?'

'Apparently,' Will said, mug by his lips, watching as Jake tore open the packet and set to the crackers. Jake was not a cravings kind of man, unless it was a post-coital need for food. And since he'd been at Amy's... 'Things still going well with Amy, then?'

'Ah, mate, what can I say? She loves Jakey-boy,' Jake responded, gripping his crotch.

Will watched him in distaste, never having understood why Jake gave his dick a pet name. Naming a car was odd enough, but to name a part of your body. Maybe it was one of those straight things that Jake always insisted he didn't understand.

'She likes a little love, then?' he asked, his smile all-innocent.

Jake removed his hand and put on a look of hurt. 'Hey, it ain't that bad, mate.'

'Funny, that's not what I remember.'

'Man, we were like thirteen. Fella grows a bit after that.'

'Well, I certainly have,' Will said, enjoying the look of offence on Jake's face. He laughed. 'Still, what is it they say?'

Jake narrowed his eyes, looking to see if Will was humouring him. Once satisfied that Will wasn't, he said, 'Well, it's one cliché that's spot on. And I use it damn well.'

'I'm sure you do.'

For a few seconds, silence just hung between them as they looked each other over. It was one of those comfortable silences that only two people who knew each other intimately could share. No need to speak, just being in the company of the other was enough. Sometimes, Will thought, it felt like they were mister and mister. He missed Jake being around as much. Not that he blamed Jake, of course. Relationships changed things, but still...

'Mike was asking after you,' Jake said suddenly.

'Cool. How is he anyway? Not seen him in a while.'

'Yeah, he's good. Still hankering for a bit of the Will sausage.'

Will rolled his eyes at that. It was an old joke. Jake liked to believe Will was interested in Mike, even though the guy was clearly straight. Once, a couple of years back, Jake had gone to great lengths to make sure he left Will and Mike alone at a table in The Chancery so they could get to know each other better. That they'd known each other as long as Jake had known Mike didn't seem to matter. After only five minutes Will could tell that Mike was happily married and had no interest whatsoever in experimenting with the gayer things of life.

'Guess I'll just have to save myself for someone else, then,' Will said.

To which Jake burst out laughing. 'Yeah, sure, like that's gonna happen!'

'It might,' Will said, pointedly he thought, but Jake seemed not to notice since he continued laughing his way into the lounge.

5. Mixed Signals

Over the lip of his cards, Jake watched Will study his own hand. This was nice. It seemed like months since the two of them had just chilled, pulled an all-nighter. When he'd told Amy about it, she had gladly agreed.

'I don't want to get between you,' she had said. 'You told me Will's been acting odd recently. Seems a good chance to find out what's up with him.' And she was right.

'You don't think I'm abandoning you, do you?'

Will looked up from the cards in his hand, and Jake could tell he'd caught his mate off guard. Will removed the Fosters can from his mouth. 'Huh?'

'Well, last couple of months my life has pretty much been Amy.'

'Oh. That.'

Something passed by Will's face, just for a moment, then it was gone. But it was long enough for Jake to notice. He wasn't sure what he was seeing, but there seemed to be a familiarity there, as if Will could relate in some way. Which would be impossible, unless...

'Why, are you abandoning me?'

'No,' Jake said. 'Never. But I've seen so little of you. And, you know, don't want you to think you're taking second place now that I'm with Amy.'

'Well, isn't that the whole point of a relationship?'

Jake sat back against the couch and rubbed his hand over his head, feeling the roughness of the stubble as his hair slowly grew back. He had to remember to shave it again tomorrow. Originally the bald look was just a thing he was trying out, but Amy liked it a lot so it was going to stay for a while. He'd probably end up missing his hair eventually, though, especially the compliments he tended to get on the colour. The ginger was so dark that it almost seemed brown in some light... or did until he shaved it off.

They were sitting on the floor in the lounge, the results of their munch littering the rug; half-empty packets of crackers, crisps and Pringles, plus a couple of empty cans. That Will had cans of lager in the fridge surprised Jake, since he got the impression that the all-nighter was a spur-of-the-moment thing. But clearly, the cans had been in the fridge for a while. Very much not a Will thing to do. That it was Fosters was a bit of a downer. For some time he'd been trying to convince Will to keep a few cans on hand just in case, but he was hoping for something a bit stronger than the dirty dishwater that was Fosters.

They were playing Canasta, and Will was so far winning. It was one of those games that could change at a moment's notice, so Jake was just waiting for the right cards. It'd happen sooner or later.

Will placed his cards on the floor and offered a smile. 'I'm glad for you. Guess there is always someone out there.' He grinned. 'Still, you honestly think Amy is settling down material?'

'Hmm, don't know about that one,' Jake said, letting out a whistle of air. 'Two months is a big deal for me, but, look at it this way, Will, we're not getting any younger. Little over five years and we're forty. Settling down has to come soon, yeah?'

'Well, forty ain't that old these days. Not like when we were kids.'

'No, this is true. But it's still forty. How long before we decide it's time to settle down? Fifty? Sixty?'

Will placed a hand on Jake's knee. 'Maybe we're going to end up in a retirement home together?'

Jake batted Will's hand away. He blinked, certain that for the briefest of seconds he saw hurt in Will's eyes then. 'You wish! No, but seriously, mate, don't you ever think about this shit? Most of the people we knew at school are either married or have kids.'

'A very few of them are even doing both, I hear.'

Jake laughed. 'Yeah, who'd have seen that coming in South West London? The most prolific area of single parents in the UK.'

'You know.'

Despite the humour, there was a definite undercurrent to their words. Jake could feel it in himself and could see it in Will's eyes. Things had changed in the last couple of months, for both of them, and it was only now, with the two of them talking like this, that Jake realised just how much. He knew what had changed in him, but what was changing in Will he had no idea. Something was different, though.

Earlier he'd been knocking for a good ten minutes before he decided to come around to the kitchen door. After a few attempts at banging on the wooden frame, he'd got Will's attention, but even then his mate seemed very distracted. Something was most definitely going on in Will's life that Jake wasn't privy to, and before the night was over he was intent on discovering what.

'We'll see how things go, but I've got a good feeling about this,' he said, continuing on about him and Amy. For now. He'd await his opportunity, then start digging.

'Well, if there are ever wedding bells, I bagsy best man.'

'Like that was ever in doubt. What about you? You feel like it's time to find a mister?'

Any answer that Will was going to give was put on hold by a sudden thump from upstairs. They both looked up, thinking the same thing. Curtis had fallen out of bed.

'I'll sort him out,' Jake said. 'You go open a couple more cans.'

He noticed the look on Will's face as he walked out of the lounge. A look of relief.

Yup, Jake thought, some digging was needed.

*

They were back in the kitchen now. It was a nice humid night, not too warm and not too cold, and so the back door was open, Jake propping up the frame while he grabbed a fag. Will was leaning against the side, the kettle boiling behind him. He watched Jake and smiled to himself. There was a new glow about his friend that he liked; relationship suited Jake, gave him a bearing that was fresh and true. If anyone had told him Jake would finally meet someone he could actually fall in love with, Will would never have believed them, and yet here he was. The warmth in his voice when he talked of Amy was unexpected, but it worked and left no doubt in Will's mind that Jake was on to a good thing.

Going away for a weekend didn't seem so bad now, with the knowledge that Jake at least had found the thing Will was looking for. By the time he returned on Sunday, Will hoped that he, too, would be feeling the same kind of glow that Jake currently enjoyed. By which time there was no way Jake could bitch him out about his internet romance.

He swallowed hard. Now was as good a time as any.

'Do you remember Jacen Bishop?' he asked, in lieu of any kind of build-up.

Jake didn't look back as he answered. 'Yeah, whatever happened to him?'

'Ended up with some high-octane bloke from what I've heard. Out living the life of the adrenalin junkie in Australia.'

'Good for him. I liked him,' Jake said, glancing in, watching Will carefully.

'So did I.'

'I remember. Still don't get why you let him go.' Jake blew smoke out into the back yard, then turned back to Will. 'Big mistake, really, eh? You guys were happy.'

'We were, but he wanted a different kind of life to what I could offer.' Will shrugged. 'But recently I've been wondering what would have happened if we'd stayed together, where would we be now?'

'You probably would have imploded by now. As you say, the life he wanted wasn't the same as you. He wanted to be out there, enjoying life; you've always been about securing your future. Fun quotient at a low.'

'You're right, I should have followed him, found the fun. Run the risk a little.'

Jake narrowed his eyes and let out a hmm. He stubbed the cigarette out on the yard wall and tossed it into the tin provided for the butts, then re-entered the kitchen.

'Come on, Will, we've known each other too long. Where's this going? You've found someone, right?'

'What? No. I... Yes, yes, I have.' Feeling the colour rush to his cheeks, Will turned away to make the coffee, readying himself for the expected chewing-out.

'About time. Tell me all.'

*

A man stood across the street from Will's house. The street was quiet, all the noise of Fulham Broadway, the so-called night life, was far enough away that it failed to spill onto Barclay Road.

Which was just as well, Stephen thought. He hated having to do this, but he made a promise to Robin, and if there was one thing Stephen knew for sure, it was that it was impossible to break a promise to Robin once it was made.

He glanced around, lifted his hoodie so it protected his face from the light of the streetlamps and crossed the road to Will's car. He pulled out a set of spare keys that he'd had copied some time ago and opened the driver's door. He looked up at the house; no sign of movement in the front room, which meant wherever Will and Jake had gone, they were still there. Probably out the back having a smoke. Or, Stephen thought with a wolfish grin, they'd finally given in to their ever-building carnal desires.

He popped the bonnet, and quickly moved around the front of the car and set to work.

*

Feeling dumb, Will took a deep breath and handed a mug to Jake. They both took a stool each and sat down. Jake just watched, waiting expectantly. Will was dreading it, although he still didn't know why.

'Well... His name's Charlie, and we've been in contact for about a month now. At first it was just small talk, silly nonsense, but just over a week ago things changed. Became more serious.'

Jake nodded. 'A month, and I'm only now just hearing about it? Have I been so wrapped up with Amy...?'

Will shook his head. 'No, course not, it's just... Guess I wanted to see if there was anything to tell first.'

'Fair.' Jake laughed lightly. 'Well, I'm all for things becoming unexpectedly serious. So, in contact? Met him through work?'

Will chewed his bottom lip. 'Not exactly. Online.'

'Oh.'

Will studied Jake's face, trying to gauge how he was really feeling about this. It was hard to say. Jake had his thinking face on, which was as inscrutable as his poker face.

'Oh...?' Will prompted.

'Well, okay, not the way I'd expect you to meet someone, but I guess it's the twenty-first century here, so okay. Have you met him yet?'

'No.'

'Oh. Please tell me you've seen more than a picture? Cause, you know, pictures often lie. For all you know it could be some dirty old bastard sending a young picture, or it could be some behemoth hiding behind a pic that isn't even him. The net's a bit on the impersonal side, loads of shit comes of it.'

'I know that, Jake, I'm not stupid.' Will stood, coming off as way more defensive than he intended. 'I've spoken to him on the phone, over webcam, the whole nine yards. He's who he says he is.'

Jake nodded again, his thinking face returning. 'You planning to meet him?'

'This weekend, as it happens. I'm going to stay at his place for a couple of—'

'Whoa there, Will, mate! You're meeting him at his? Wouldn't some neutral, *public*, place be better? Okay, so you've Skyped with him, whoopy shit, that doesn't mean you know him.'

Will shook his head and walked over to the sink. 'I knew you'd react like this. Do you think I'm dumb or something? I'm almost thirty-five, mate, I know my own mind and I know how to judge people. If this wasn't real, do you honestly think I'd be pursuing it?'

'Normally I'd say no. But...' Jake let out a sigh of frustration. 'I need a fag.' He got back up and stepped out into the yard.

Will followed him. When he stepped out he received a glare from Jake, but it wasn't anger, it was concern.

'Are you sure about this?'

'Sure? As much as I can be, yes. Remember what you said about Jacen? About me taking some risks? Well this is it, Jake. I need to do this. Every day my life is the same, I work, I juggle the money, I make a profit, I end up bailing my family out of their shit. I'm constantly dumped upon by everyone.' Will let out a breath of air, and looked up at the night sky. 'I'm buckling under it all.'

'No kidding.' Jake placed a hand on Will's shoulder and the two men looked each other in the eye. 'I love you, Will, you know that. We're brothers, man. Of course I want you to be happy. Not sure I understand this internet romance thing, but if you need to do this, then cool. You do it.' He smiled, and the two of them drew closer. 'Maybe one day the four of us can go for a drink together.'

Will grinned. 'That would be cool.'

The two of them hugged abruptly. Will closed his eyes and felt something he hadn't for a very long time...

And it was something, judging by Jake's own physical reaction, that he felt too.

They pulled apart and cleared their throats.

'I think I need to go for a pee,' Jake said, and quickly rushed into the house.

Will stood there. Maybe it was just sexual frustration on his part. He hoped so. But that didn't explain Jake's own boner...

'Fuck,' he said. 'I so need to spend the night with Charlie.'

*

Will struggled to clip Curtis into the booster seat, a task not made easy by Curtis' constant fidgeting. The kid had been in a bad mood all morning, ever since Jake had awoken him. Will suspected it had something to do with Jimmy coming back soon; Curtis often got antsy whenever he knew his dad was due back. After his weekend away, Will decided, he was going to look into it.

He felt quite fresh this morning, himself. Jake had left earlier, heading to work, after an all-nighter that had ended about three in the morning. Nothing was said about their 'hug', which suited Will fine. It wasn't something he really wanted to think about, let alone talk about.

Some sleep was had, but looking at Jake it seemed not to be enough for him. Will, however, felt great. No doubt due to their discussion last night. Knowing Jake had his back created a safe feeling in Will, and he had woken up deciding that a lot was going to change when he returned on Sunday.

No more sitting about on the side-lines and letting the shit go down in his family. Time to take a stand and be counted.

Between now and then he resigned to not let anything get him down or pile on him.

Then, naturally, his car refused to start.

6. Every Contingency

Will pulled the lounge curtains to; there was just too much sunlight that morning. He blinked away the spots and shook his head.

'I don't get it,' he said into the phone. 'My eyes aren't too good in bright sun usually, but this past week...'

'Guess I'll just have to keep you in the shadows all weekend,' Charlie said on the other end of the line.

Will grinned. 'Oh yeah?'

'Yeah. In fact, maybe we'll just never leave the house.'

Will wanted to say that was probably a little too fast, but it wasn't like they hadn't done anything over Skype. Charlie had certainly seen Will's scar at the top of his left leg, barely inches away from other usually private areas, and...

Will swallowed, feeling a stirring in those areas at the thought of it.

'I suppose I do have a lot of energy to burn,' Will said, keeping his tone light and playful. 'And you don't drive...'

'But I do ride.'

Will smirked. 'Oh, I just bet you do. Anyway,' he added, looking around. 'I need to clear up and get everything packed.'

'Just think, in a few short hours you'll be with me.'

'Finally.'

'Yes. Finally.'

It may have only been a month, but when you couldn't be in the physical presence of your lover, those weeks seemed such a long time. Will was still a little nervous, but he was excited too. It was kind of thrilling to step outside his safe space.

'Okay, lover,' Charlie said. 'Let me know when you're on the train.'

'Will do.' Will stopped himself just short of saying 'love you' before he said, 'Bye for now.' He may feel like he was falling in love, but to openly tell Charlie... That was a slightly bigger step than Will was ready for. At least until he was actually in Charlie's embrace.

He left the lounge to make himself another cuppa, grinning like the proverbial cat with the cream, and sent a text to Jake.

Wakey wakey sleepy head. Today's the day!

He stopped before hitting send, his smile fading. He glanced up at the ceiling, imagining that he heard Curtis turn in his sleep. The boy would be awake soon. Poor kid, he'd spent more time at Will's this past week than he had with his parents. Or maybe that wasn't such a bad thing for him...? On the one hand, a child needed its parents, but one the other, when those parents were Ren and Jimmy...

Will took a deep breath, his mind returning to something he'd been thinking about a lot the last week. Even longer, if he was honest with himself. He felt sure about it, but he still wondered if he was doing the right thing. Or was he going too far? Either way...

Popping over? Need to talk about something. Important.

*

Frederick looked at the phone in his hand and smiled.

It was almost time. In a few hours Willem would be en route to Southend, and then...

For the first time in two hundred years he actually felt nervous. The last time he had felt anything close to it was when he'd set off for Moldavia, for his fateful meeting with the Ancient. It made sense. Two of the biggest moments in his whole life (in his many lives!), both connected by a single goal... To reveal the truth to his people once and for all.

He crossed his room and walked the long corridor to Celeste's private rooms. But before he could knock, a voice behind him spoke.

'Private call, or can anyone butt in?'

He turned to face Eryn. 'Is anything private to you?'

'As one of the Three, no.'

'That's what you think.' Frederick turned his back on her, knocked, and entered upon Celeste's instruction. But not before glancing back at Eryn, winking, and making sure the door closed firmly behind him.

*

'Na-na-na, come on!'

Jake stirred at the opening thumping beats of Rihanna's *S&M*. He reached over Amy's sleeping form, careful not to disturb her, and espied the clock on the side. It was nine o'clock. Which wasn't too bad, he guessed, at least he had a little bit of a lay-in. He just hoped it wasn't Mikey sending him a message saying he was wanted in work after all; this day off was well deserved, and Amy and he had plans for it.

He picked up the phone and opened the message.

Seconds later he was lying on his back, looking at the ceiling of his bedroom. He had forgotten that today was the day, and now that the text reminded him, the worries surfaced.

At first, he wasn't sure if it was right to talk to anyone about it, and most of Wednesday he spent quietly working on the site, his usual chatty self left behind at Will's. But when he'd seen Amy that night everything had come out, and Amy proved to be a good sounding board. She took everything in and didn't offer any advice, until the next day when she told him what she thought of the situation. Her viewpoint had allayed his fears for a time, but now that it was Friday and the moment was almost upon him...

'Who was it?' asked a slurred voice beside him.

Jake smiled, and rolled onto his side so he could look down at Amy's morning face. She opened her eyes slowly, and smiled up at him, and once again he realised how lucky he was. How many women looked just as good in the morning as they did during the sweat-filled love making session last thing at night?

'Will. He's asked me to pop over before he heads off, wants to talk about something.'

Amy lifted herself up onto her elbow. 'Last minute change of mind?'

'Not Will. I wish. He's not the kind of guy to change his mind once he's decided on a course of action. Well, unless it involves his sister.'

Amy nodded slowly and sat up, reaching for the little cabinet on her side of the bed, and the glass of water sitting atop it. She always slept with a glass of water waiting for her, and first thing she took a sip. She said it helped her start her day, rehydrate her sleeping body before she made it to the kitchen and broke her night long fast. She took the glass to her lips and tilted it back, in the process knocking the duvet down, revealing her pert breasts. She noticed, but didn't bother covering them again, and Jake was glad. It was a great sight to wake up to.

'You going over?' she asked, and Jake nodded slowly. 'Still worried?'

He looked into her blue eyes; they carried their usual playful edge, a hint of naughtiness behind them. Already Jake could tell it was going to be a good morning.

'Of course,' he said, getting his mind back on track, no easy task with her sitting beside him like that. 'My best mate is off to rendezvous with some random bloke he's only known via the net. I think that's cause for concern.'

'I suppose. But we were strangers when we first met, too. Is Will's situation so different?'

Jake had thought much about this, and he totally got what Amy was saying, and partly he agreed with her. But nonetheless...

'But I could see you, and if it didn't work out I was still in my hometown, surrounded by friends. Will's going out to a town he doesn't know; what if it turns out that Charlie is some nutter?'

'Extreme case scenario, wouldn't you say, Jacob?'

Jake couldn't help but smile, there was something about the way Amy used his full name that made him feel relaxed. 'I'm probably worrying about nothing.'

'Yes,' Amy agreed, guiding her free hand down his chest. Jake let out a shiver and Amy raised an eyebrow as her cold hand cupped his balls. 'Let's work out some of that tension before you go and express your concerns to Will.'

Jake oohed and aahed, glancing at the clock, feeling a stiffening down below. 'You know what, I think I can be tempted.'

*

Message received, Will flipped his phone closed and placed it on the kitchen counter. Jake was about ten minutes away. Will walked into the lounge, mug in one hand, the morning newspaper in the other.

Curtis came running into his knees as he entered the lounge, almost causing him to spill his hot coffee. 'Hey,' he said, steadying Curtis with his hand while simultaneously trying not to drop the newspaper. 'Steady on there, buddy, you'll do yourself a mischief.'

Curtis looked up at him, his brown eyes smiling out of his bronze face. Will shook his head, as usual unable to resist his nephew. 'Tick tock,' Curtis said.

'Yeah, okay, let me just put this down or it'll burn you.' Obligingly, Curtis stepped aside and allowed his uncle into the room. He placed the mug on the mantelpiece and flopped the paper onto his chair, then turned to Curtis. 'Come on, then.'

He bent down and grabbed the boy by the ankles, then quickly flipped him upside down, swaying him gently from side to side. As he swayed, Curtis cried out 'tick tock' at the top of his little lungs, laughing with every ounce of his being. Will couldn't help but laugh at this, and wondered if he would have been as happy had some giant decided to do the same to him. Probably not, but then, he supposed, a thirty-five-year-old man was not as supple as a two-and-a-half-year-old boy. He gently swung Curtis over to the couch and let him go. The boy landed softly on the cushions, his arms and legs flailing, giggling uncontrollably.

'Right, little mista,' Will said, between his own laughter, 'go and watch Upsy Daisy, or no yums for you.'

Curtis scrambled onto the rug in the middle of the room and planted himself in front of the TV. Once again Will was amazed at how sharp Curtis' mind was; was it normal for a kid his age to understand so well? Will wasn't so sure, but he was certain that kids weren't as intelligent back in his day.

He grimaced as he left the room for the kitchen. *Back in his day.* He sounded like an old man.

Getting away for a weekend was so needed.

He stopped at the open backdoor, feeling the cold air brushing against his extremities, and shuddered. It was almost ten and he was still walking about in his robe, having spent most of the past hour getting his stuff together for his weekend away. That, and keeping Curtis amused. For him to reach this time of the morning and not even have a shower was unheard of; even on his off days he tended to be dressed by nine, and it was now *forty minutes* after the nine o'clock! Still, he allowed himself the luxury of taking things easy that morning on account of his not going to be home again for two days.

He took the now soldiered sandwiches in to Curtis and placed them before the kid, who took one of the soldiers and stuffed it into his mouth, his eyes never leaving the TV upon which Upsy Daisy was running through the Night Garden looking for her bed, which had decided to roll away again.

Smiling, Will straightened himself up and headed for the front door. When he opened it he found Jake there, hand raised as if about to knock.

Jake did a double take, and frowned. 'What is this, *Sixth Sense?*'

'Yeah,' Will said, and winked. 'I see gay people.'

'Uh huh.' Jake smacked Will upside the head and entered the hallway. 'Your eyes clearly need testing, then, mate,' he said, and carried on into the lounge. 'Hey, champ!'

Will closed the door with a smirk, after a quick wave to some random passer-by who happened to look up in time to see this rather good-looking bloke standing in the doorway with nothing on but a bathrobe. The old woman, who either blushed very easily or was heavily made up, quickly looked away embarrassed. Will wasn't too sure if she was embarrassed for him or her, but decided to not bother asking. He returned to the lounge, but got as far as the doorway before stopping, and just watched his best mate and nephew as they played.

That was what Will loved about Jake; he always came across as a bit of a tough-nut, the kind of guy who was always good humoured around those he liked, but not the sort of person you'd want to cross. The shaved head added to this effect, and it was a look Will was beginning to get used to. Despite all this, Jake could be the gentlest soul in the world, amazingly compassionate and considerate, and his tactility with young children was beyond reproach.

Now they were rolling on the floor, Curtis on top, arms held high claiming he was the winner. Jake offered Will a wink.

'Coffee?' Will asked, still smiling.

'Good call,' Jake replied.

Once Jake was able to extricate himself from Curtis, he joined Will in the kitchen and plonked himself on his usual stool by the back door. He pulled out a cigarette and lit it.

'So, what's the what? I doubt you called me here just to admire my gorgeous looks.'

Jake was in a good mood, but Will couldn't resist poking fun at him. He turned from the kettle and looked Jake up and down. The tight jeans Jake wore were doing him no favours, pressed as they were against his not so impressive crotch. 'You wish. I like my men to satisfy me.'

'Yeah, yeah, you can't fool me. I'm just too much man for you. One day you'll have to admit it.'

Will laughed. 'Okay, one day, I promise. Until then, I need to talk to you about Curtis.'

Jake's good humour left him abruptly and he sat up straight, casting a quick glance to the hallway beyond. 'What about him?'

Will held up a hand, and said quickly, 'Don't worry, he's not been harmed or anything like that. I'm just concerned for his wellbeing.' He let Jake relax a little before asking, 'How many times has Curtis stayed here in the last two weeks?'

Jake thought about this. 'Three, four?'

'Three, right. Two of those nights have been in the last three days. I don't know what's going on with Ren, and right now I don't much care, but a kid Curtis' age needs stability, not to be pulled from pillar to post.'

'Agreed. So, what do you suggest?'

'I'm not sure, exactly, but I'm seriously thinking of bringing the Social in.'

Jake's eyes widened in surprise, although Will wasn't sure why. It was a natural conclusion after the last few weeks.

'That would be a seriously bad move, man, get them involved and Lawrencia could end up losing Curtis.'

'Want to explain to me how that's a bad thing?'

Jake shook his head, and threw his cigarette into the back yard, without even trying to stub it out first. 'How's this for a start; if Curtis ends up in Care you might never even get to see him again. He gets put up for fostering, next thing you know he's lost in the system, just another unwanted child. Name changed. How long before you lose track of him?'

That hadn't occurred to Will; he had only been thinking that Curtis was in danger around Jimmy and, unfortunately by extension, his sister. 'Worst case...'

'Scenario? Yeah, I'm hearing that a lot. Someone needs to consider these eventualities, Will, because it seems like your brain isn't functioning properly at the moment.'

'Oh, come on, just because I'm trying to get out of my comfort zone a bit?'

Jake didn't answer, instead he stood up and left the kitchen. Will narrowed his eyes, but followed nonetheless. The two of them stopped by the lounge and looked in on Curtis, who had fallen asleep watching CBeebies.

'Tell me, Will, do you really want to lose that kid? Cause I know I don't.'

Will stepped back and rested against the wall. He closed his eyes and let out a breath of air. Now he thought about it, Jake was right. He opened his eyes and looked at Jake, who was still looking into the lounge. Jake loved Curtis; as far as Curtis knew Jake was as much his uncle as Will was. Blood didn't matter in this case; it was the familial bond that counted.

'What do you suggest?' he asked.

Jake never took his eyes off Curtis. 'Speak to her, work something out. I don't know the details, but there is shit going on you're not aware of, mate, and I'd lay money on Lawrencia waiting for help from her big brother.' He looked back at Will, and there was something in his eyes that made Will believe him. 'Maybe you can become his legal guardian, temporarily at least, until she gets rid of that dead weight?'

Now it was Will's turn to be surprised. 'Come on, really? Even if Ren did agree to that, how can I look after him full time? My workload is...'

'Not insurmountable. Way you tell it Steve is amazing at his job, so I'm sure he could take a whole load of weight off your shoulders there.'

'I suppose.' Will mulled it over, and he had to admit the idea did have much potential.

Jimmy would never stand for it, but Jake would no doubt happily take care of that, and once Curtis was out of harm's way Will didn't care two shits about what happened to Jimmy. Getting Lawrencia to agree, though, that would be a tough one. She'd take it as a personal attack.

'Okay, let me think this over, and when I get back we'll talk more.'

'Cool.'

Will smiled, glad to have come closer to some kind of resolution there. He brushed past Jake and scooped Curtis into his arms. He was due a midday nap anyway, and ten past ten was close enough.

'I'm taking him upstairs, you coming? I need to get my shit together before I have a shower anyhow.'

Not waiting for an answer and knowing Jake would follow, Will left the room and took to the stairs. When he came back out of Curtis' room, he found Jake at the bottom of the second flight of stairs.

'Will you keep an eye on Curtis while I'm away?' Will asked.

'Of course I will, as best I can,' Jake replied, leading the way up to Will's bedroom. He sat down on the edge of the bed while Will made himself busy. 'This is going to end badly, you know.'

'Probably,' Will said, opening his underwear drawer. 'But I have to do this, for Curtis.'

'No, I mean this little weekend away. Haven't you seen *Hard Candy*?'

Will pulled out a fresh pair of socks and a pair of his favourite SPY Henry Lau sports briefs, designed with that extra bit of lift in mind. The wonder bra of men's underwear.

'Well, yeah, since it's my DVD. And, okay, I can understand how meeting someone I've only known from the net can seem a little odd, but I'm not a kid. I *can* handle myself.'

'Sure, cause you're so tough.' Jake let out a sigh and looked to the floor. 'Come on, Will, we're in London. Social capital of the UK; you must be able to find someone. Not like London is short on gay men.'

'I imagine that's true,' Will said, now looking into his wardrobe for suitable clothes to make a good first impression on Charlie. That they'd seen each other via webcam meant nothing. In person was a whole new ball game. 'Problem is, I don't get out enough to meet them. You know this. If I'm not swamped in work, I'm looking after Curtis, or I'm bailing Ren out of the latest mess, *or* I'm running around after Mother.'

'We go out.'

'Right. And you know there are so many gay men in The Chancery. Jake, mate, be glad for me, please. Sure, this could be a complete disaster, I know that, but on the other hand things could work out really well. Charlie could be my version of Amy.'

'Great comparison there, bud.'

'You know what I'm saying.' With a sigh Will threw himself on the bed, stretching out. 'This life of mine is doing my nut in, man. Steve was spot on; I need to get out of my own little box.'

'You discussed this with Steve?'

'Yeah. Why?'

Jake shook his head. 'Nothing.'

Will watched him a moment. 'I seem to recall you said the same thing a few years back when I was with Jacen.'

Jake turned around and stretched out on the bed next to Will. When they were young they'd spent hours in a similar fashion, laid out on one or the other's bed. Jake chatting about the latest hot girl, while Will mooned over the new boy in school who caught his eye. Mooning over was the right phrase, since the only other boy he'd ever had on his bed was Jake and, other than a brief fiddle, nothing had ever happened between them.

'Same shit, different day, right?' Jake said. 'Think your life is any different from everyone else in London? We all do it, guy. Work, go for a drink, eat, sleep, work, go for a drink. Same cycle.'

'You have fun. You always have fun!'

'Yeah, because I don't let myself get too caught up in the shit. Life's for living.'

'Right,' Will said, flicking Jake's arm. 'And that's what I'm trying to do, find a way to live *my* life for a change, and not my family's.'

Jake shrugged, and Will could tell he was folding. 'Well, maybe. But there has to be a better way than with a stranger.'

'Charlie's not a stranger, not anymore. And was Amy any less a stranger two months back?'

Jake sat up. 'That's exactly what she said.'

'See, I knew I always liked her.' Will sat up too, and nudged Jake with his shoulder. 'Come on, cheer up, bro. If there's really anything between Charlie, like we think there is, then we need to meet. See if we've got the same chemistry in person.'

'And a bit of fun in the sack wouldn't go amiss, either, eh?' Jake asked, his old mischievous tones returning.

Will glared at him, but he couldn't be serious any longer. So he laughed.

'Well, yeah, of course that would be nice. Gay men have needs too.'

'Oh well, if that's all there is to it,' Jake said, placing a hand on Will's leg. 'What say I just give you a quick wank now? Get rid of that frustration for you.'

For a few seconds Will actually thought Jake was serious, and an old fantasy rushed to the forefront of his mind. He quickly stood, keeping his back to Jake so that his boner wouldn't be evident. 'You son of a bitch, nearly had me hard then,' he said, adding a bit of extra levity for good effect, filling his head with random images guaranteed to bring his dick under control.

'Thanks, nice mental image there.'

'Best mental image you've had in a while I reckon.'

'Don't need one, mate, Amy does me quite nicely. Do you really find these things comfortable?'

Will turned to see Jake brandishing his sport briefs. He snatched them off Jake. 'Very.'

'I'm more of a boxer man, myself, prefer to let things swing freely.'

'Yeah, cause you ain't got much to swing. People like me need to keep it all together, you know?' Will gathered up the rest of his clothes and left his room. He heard Jake's footfalls on the steps behind him. 'I'm getting my shower. Ren should be here soon, so if you want to wait around, no problem. But,' he said, stopping by the bathroom door, 'unless you want to watch me throw one off myself, you might want to wait downstairs.'

Jake screwed up his face. 'Thanks, I think I'll pass.'

Will watched Jake descend the second flight of stairs, then he turned and headed into the bathroom. Sometimes Jake was such an easy target.

*

'Don't let me down.'

'I won't,' Stephen said. 'Like I ever have.'

'True. Very well,' Robin said, his voice low as if he were trying to speak in a crowded room and didn't want to be heard. 'I shall have Anna meet up with you, bring you some Red Source.'

Before Stephen could say thank you, Robin hung up.

Stephen remained standing, looking out of the office window over North End Road. It was busy as usual, people hustling and bustling around, going from shop to shop. He tried to not think about what he had done, how he felt about it, because he knew if he thought too hard he would feel guilty.

Will had always been so good to him, but Robin... The promises Robin made, the things he had shown Stephen. Eight years now...

*

'Bro, that was just... wow!' Stephen looked up at the glass faced tower, unable to wipe the smile off his face. Only seconds ago both he and his mate were at the top of the Canary Wharf Tower and now they were both standing in the square below, surrounded by a cheering crowd who stood behind barriers some distance away.

'Express elevator to hell, right?'

'God yeah.' Stephen laughed, and took a deep breath. 'Shit. BASE jumping is just... Shit yeah! Can't get much more crazy than that!'

'That a challenge?'

'Fuck yeah!' Stephen said and held his hand out, which his mate grasped with equal fervour, their thumbs linking. That's what Stephen loved about Robin, always throwing out the next challenge, which he knew Stephen would have to accept. Some called him an adrenalin junkie, and maybe they were right. Fact was Stephen didn't want to waste his life; he had to live on the edge. He'd almost died in a car accident when he was a kid, and since then it seemed foolish to waste his second chance.

'Dude, we should probably clear up the parachutes,' Robin said. 'Before our adoring fans want our autographs.' He nodded at the crowds.

Stephen looked over and laughed. 'Yeah, extreme sports, extreme fans. Which reminds me, those twins from last night... erm, Karen and Anne? Did you get their numbers?'

'Sorry, mate, forgot,' Robin said, as he started work on gathering the parachute off the ground. 'You know me, fuck 'em and leave 'em. No time for action replays.'

'Not always true,' Stephen said with a wink.

Robin laughed at this, and playfully punched Stephen's shoulder. 'But I've never fucked you.'

'Everything but, though.'

'Too extreme for you?' Robin asked, that old wicked glint in his brown eyes, one eyebrow raised.

'You wish.'

'So, tonight then, yeah?'

Stephen shook his head, laughing. 'Yeah, you're on.'

*

Stephen swung his legs over, and with a painful sting in his groin he managed to sit on the edge of the roof next to Robin, who smiled at him, then looked out from the top of Michael Stewart House. From their vantage point at the peak of Clem Atlee Estate they could see across Fulham, out past Charing Cross Hospital and into Hammersmith. The flyover across the Broadway was clearly visible, although they could barely make out the odd car. A good view, but it was chilly. Fortunately, due to their very own version of extreme indoor sports, and the subsequent climbing onto the roof, Stephen didn't feel much of that chill. His muscles were sore, his body warm, he was also in some pain. But it was a nice pain.

'It'll probably go septic by the morning,' he said.

Robin shrugged. 'Not necessarily. Depends on how well you heal.'

'Well enough,' Stephen said, gently pulling the crotch of his jeans away from his now very sensitive genitals. 'Still, that was... Where did you learn that?'

'Jassy, a small place in Moldavia.'

'Right. You've travelled a lot,' Stephen said, having forgotten the amount of places Robin had mentioned in a first-hand-experience kind of way.

They'd only known each other about four months, met in a pub off Oxford Street. Stephen noticed something in Robin he'd found very familiar, and decided to introduce himself. Soon found out they had much in common, including a love for extreme sports. Of course, back in November Stephen had no idea that Robin liked to take those extreme sports into the bedroom. But hey, Stephen was up for trying anything once, and that first night when Robin had applied pressure *there* Stephen had almost fallen to his knees. It had hurt at first, but then the adrenalin kicked in, the endorphins were released, and he found himself incredibly turned on by the pain. It reminded him of the time he'd got his back tattooed, also an incredibly erotic kind of pain.

Now here they were. Stephen would never call himself gay, nor Robin come to that, but they had developed a rather interesting friendship, one with very few boundaries. It wasn't about sex, none of it was, it was about the rush, the high they both got. Be it with each other or with women involved, it didn't much matter. What mattered was the end result; the high!

'What if I told you that you're still missing out on the biggest high of them all?' Robin asked, almost as if he had read Stephen's mind.

'Then I'd say let's do it, man!'

Robin nodded his head slowly. 'Right, okay, but I need to show you something first.'

'What?'

Robin looked at Stephen and winked. Then, without preamble, he flung himself off the roof.

For a second, unable to believe his eyes, Stephen continued to look in the spot Robin had occupied, then he lowered his head, his heart beating faster than it had ever beaten before, and saw something that he just couldn't accept.

Several stories below, on the grass, Robin was clambering to his feet. At first he seemed to have little balance, but Stephen figured that might have had something to do with the way Robin's left leg was completely out of joint. He shook his head, wondering at the way he was viewing this. It was abstract, unreal. Yet...

Robin popped his leg back into place and beckoned Stephen to join him.

Stephen swallowed. Right, BASE jumping was one thing, but to do it without a parachute... He was an adrenalin junkie, sure, but not insane.

*

In the time it took for him to walk to the ground floor, two things changed in Stephen. One, his legs had decided to work properly again, the alternate stiffness (from the extreme exertion) and shakiness (from the shock of seeing one's best mate commit a failed suicide) had subsided. Two, his mind had settled on anger. The shock, which probably hadn't gone totally, had crystallized.

He found Robin still outside, now sitting on the bar that ran the length of the wall at the edge of the grass. He had his back to Stephen, looking across at the Fulham Pools on the opposite side of Lillie Road.

'What the fuck was that, man?' Stephen wanted to know.

Still Robin didn't turn. Stephen slowed his walk. Something was different about Robin, the way he sat. There was new strength to him, not to say that Robin had ever proven weak, but he sat like a different man. The kind of man you didn't want to fuck with.

'Listen, how did you do that?' Stephen stopped a few feet away.

'Come sit with me, and I'll tell you.'

Even Robin's voice sounded different. He sounded like an older man. Stephen took a deep breath. He couldn't back away now; he had to know how Robin had managed to jump off that block of flats and survive. So he did as he was told. He climbed the wall and sat next to Robin.

For a moment neither spoke, they both looked out to the empty road. Fortunate that it was half three in the morning, no spectators to witness Robin's miracle BASE jump.

Robin turned his face slightly, and the person Stephen saw looking at him was not Robin. It had nothing to do with the cuts on his face, it was more to do with the way the face sat. The features seemed harder somehow, more serious, no trace of a smile at all. Stephen didn't know what to think, but he was sure he was not looking at the nineteen-year-old Northern lad he'd known for four months.

'Do you still want the biggest high ever?'

Again Stephen swallowed. He really did want it. It's what he lived for. All the hours he put in at work at the coffee shop; he hadn't become a manager at twenty-two just because he loved his job. Will paid him a good wage, more than enough to pay for his extreme life style. And he'd done it all, every extreme sport that had been invented he'd given a go, found new ways to push, to make the rush even more intoxicating. Now Robin was offering him something else entirely...

'What is it?'

'My blood, Stephen. It's special, keeps me alive. Forever.' At this Robin smiled, but it wasn't the wide 'here comes the rush' smile he usually had. This was more ironic. 'That's how I survived.'

'Forever? Uh-huh, so you're what, a vampire now?'

'Your word, not mine.'

'This is crazy.' Stephen wanted to laugh, but what he'd just witnessed... 'Well, what word would you use?' He shook his head. 'Insane. I'm going insane, must be. Vampires don't exist.'

'Again, your word.'

'I can't think of any other word for someone who feeds another their blood.'

Robin sighed, disappointed. 'What a narrow world you live in. I expected better of you.'

'Sorry. It's just... You want to give me your blood. I'm not taking your blood. Vampire or not, I don't know what you might have.'

Robin raised an eyebrow, and for the first time, without the shadow of the brow covering it, Stephen saw that Robin's right eye was extremely bloodshot. Well, he *had* fallen from a great height, something was bound to be damaged. 'If I had anything, don't you think you would have caught it by now?'

'Good point. But still...'

'Then perhaps you'd like to sample the goods?'

Stephen wasn't too sure about that, but before he could decide, Robin moved. Fast. Faster than it took them both to jump from Canary Wharf. Stephen's eyes went wide as Robin forced his mouth open. Robin's wrist was a gash of blood, torn open by an incredibly long thumbnail. No, not a nail, it was if a talon made of bone had sprouted from the tip of Robin's thumb! Stephen barely had time to take any of this in, before Robin's blood poured down his throat.

Robin whipped his arm away and Stephen fell back onto the grass. He lay there for a while, feeling his heart beating so fast, the blood whizzing around his body, adrenalin kicking in. He jumped to his feet in one swift movement, eyes darting about. He espied the playhouse in the park outside the Pools, and before he knew it, he was across the road and standing on top of the play house, balancing perfectly on the tiny roof.

'Wow. This is the shit!' he said, his voice sounding loud in his ears.

Robin leapt the fence and walked through the park. 'Well?'

'This is just...' Balance suddenly gone, Stephen tumbled and landed on his arse beside the playhouse. Robin was looking down at him; he offered a smile and his hand. For a brief second Stephen was looking down at himself, looking up at Robin, eyes glazed over. Then he changed. It was not Stephen he was looking at but an old man, incredibly old, wizened skin like bronze. He sniffed. Something was burning...

'Come back to me, Stephen,' a voice said.

The smell faded, and once again he was looking up at Robin, who effortlessly pulled him to his feet. 'What was that? I was...'

'In one of my memories. A long, long time ago... in Moldavia.'

'Your memories?' Stephen shook his head, trying to get that image out of his mind. 'Who was that man? How was I in your...'

'His name was Wamukota, the oldest of my people. And it's the blood, Stephen, it's always the blood. Our life source.' Robin offered a smile. 'The effect becomes more pronounced each time, the buzz better, and every time a different memory.' A beat. 'Want more?'

'Robin, I...' Stephen didn't know what to say. What was being offered was...

'Robin. One name in a long list.' Robin smiled. 'You'll understand. Now, do you want more?'

'God yes!' Stephen replied without compunction.

Robin nodded, the bemused expression slipping off his face like oil. 'Then we trade. I will give you as much as you like, but I need you to do something important for me.'

Stephen shrugged. 'Hey, Rob, there's always a price, right?'

'Quite so.' Robin took a step back, and for a moment the light from the lamp outside the park flashed on his face and Stephen saw the truth. Robin's right eye was not bloodshot, it was transparent, and he could see the blood flowing behind it. But the left, that was brown still... Robin blinked and reached for his eye. 'Ah yes, I lost one of my contacts when I landed. Not to worry.' He removed the lens from his left eye, and looked directly at Stephen. With matching transparent eyes. 'Do we have a deal, then? My blood for your help...?'

*

And, of course, Stephen had said yes. It was many years before Robin had asked for anything, years of Stephen taking Red Source, becoming addicted to the high it gave him, the promise of eternal life. And the things he had since learned, the things Robin had shown him.

But then the price came. Will. Robin had plans for Will, and Stephen's help was required.

Stephen thought of the damage he had done to Will's car, which had forced Will to book train tickets instead. Tickets for today.

'Sorry, Will,' he said, trying not to think of what Robin was going to do when Will reached Southend.

7. The Big Goodbye

The sound of the doorbell brought Will out of the shower fifteen minutes later. He wrapped a towel around his torso as he emerged, stopping at the top of the stairs, his body still dripping wet. He called out to Jake, having to raise his voice just to be heard over the TV.

He emerged from the lounge and glanced up the stairs. 'Hey, sexy, been thinking about me?'

'Just get the door, man,' Will said, rolling his eyes, checking to make sure the towel wasn't too tight.

When Ren entered the house, Will felt his heart sink. She looked haggard, sleep deprived; an imitation of his sister. Her appearance only deepened his resolve to sort things out once the weekend was done with.

She looked up at him, no smile forthcoming, her deep brown eyes angry. 'Where's my boy?'

'Sleeping,' Will answered, then reconsidered when he heard sound coming from Curtis' room. 'Well, he was until a certain person who shall remain nameless, *Jake*, decided to turn my lounge into a cinema.'

'Okay, okay,' Jake said, starting to climb the stairs, 'I can take a hint.'

Will didn't respond to this, neither did Lawrencia. Instead she headed for the kitchen. 'I'll put the kettle on.'

'Sure, help yourself,' Will grumbled and turned back to the bathroom. Before he even managed to step inside he felt a slap on his towel-covered backside.

'Nice ass.'

Will stopped, deciding there was a way to get Jake back one better. He turned and pulled his towel off. 'Yeah, but you know this is better,' he said, jiggling his bits.

*

A short time later, he stopped at the bottom of the stairs and placed his holdall and rucksack on the floor, before planting himself on the bottom step to put his new trainers on. A pair of navy Vans, somewhat more casual and bulkier than his usual footwear, but it completed his new ensemble nicely. Once done he headed to the kitchen, but stopped to poke his head into the lounge where Curtis and Jake were playing.

They were lying on the floor, playing one of Curtis' favourite games; Daleks versus Autobots. Jake was holding what Will liked to call a Teletubby Dalek, one of the bright primary colour Daleks introduced into *Doctor Who* last year, doing his best 'exterminate' impression, while Curtis was playing Optimus Prime. It looked like the Dalek was going to lose, what with both the Dalek and Jake's hand being pummelled by the red and blue Autobot leader.

Jake looked up, shaking his stinging hand. He blinked. 'Whoa. Where's my buddy gone?'

'Funny. As I said, time to live my own life a bit.'

'So I see. Hope he's worth it.'

Will looked down at himself, then smiled at Jake. 'He is.' Jake smiled back, and Will asked; 'Lawrencia out the back then?'

'Yep,' Jake said, and watched Will disappear down the hallway.

Once he had gone, Jake's smile faded. It was stupid, but the sudden change in clothes was like a final nail on the coffin of the Will he knew. He couldn't shake the feeling that he was losing his best friend somehow, and that the person who was going to return on Sunday would be some imposter, walking around with the same memories but with none of the character or bearing.

Jake took a deep breath.

Worst case scenario, he reminded himself, seeing Amy's tender eyes looking at him.

Will would be okay, she seemed to say, and Jake nodded, hoping she was right.

*

Will found Ren sitting on the small wall that lined the grass in the back yard, her coat wrapped about herself. He inhaled deeply, enjoying the fresh March air, and placed his sunglasses on. He glanced at his watch. He had about half an hour before he needed to be on the Tube.

'Don't start, Billy,' Ren said, looking up as he approached her.

He wasn't going to, instead he was going to try the talk-to-her tactic that Jake had suggested, but her tone immediately put him on the offensive.

'Why not? What the hell is going on with you? This is the second time Curtis has stayed here in the last three days. You can't keep on dumping him, it's not fair.'

'What else can I do?'

'Oh, I don't know, how about stay home with him? Bollocks to Jimmy; he wants to travel the country dealing his crap, let him. Curtis is your first responsibility.'

'You think I don't know this?' she asked, and sniffed. Will could see it now; stage two, the water works. He wasn't having it any more. 'I love him, Billy, don't you understand that? I know Jimmy's a twat and can't do anything right, but I love him. I *need* him.'

Will snorted his disbelief. 'And that's just bullshit. How can anyone need that kind of pond scum? He's done nothing but destroy you, Ren. I don't know what happened in Manchester, but the girl who came back...' He threw his hands up in exasperation. 'Why am I even bothering to say all this? It's all repeats.'

'You don't understand, you never did.' Ren wiped her eyes, but Will made no attempt to move closer. 'He's a good man inside, and he loves me. And he adores Curtis.'

'Right, that's why he pawns all Curtis' toys to pay off his debts? Ren, if he loved you so much he'd find a way to stop this crap. But all he does is get in deeper, and drags you down with him. There are some serious nutters out there, how long do you think it'll be before he gets tangled up in them?'

'Even Jimmy isn't that thick.'

'Sure, you could have fooled me.'

For a moment nothing more was said. She remained sitting, wiping her nose with the back of her hand, looking even more pathetic with each passing second. He stood there, watching her, his arms folded defensively. He narrowed his eyes, listening to the sounds of Jake and Curtis playing. Jake was right, the kid would be so much better living here with him. Finally, Ren looked back up from the concrete yard, and Will knew what was coming.

'Fuck,' he said. 'How much this time?'

'Six hundred.'

'What?' Will couldn't believe his ears; even his sister had never asked for so much before.

'We'll pay you back.'

'Right, like you have done in the past, yeah?'

At this Ren jumped to her feet. 'Fine, I'll just fuck off now, shall I? I'll take Curtis and if anything happens to us, you'll be happy knowing you could have helped. If I wanted the guilt trip I could have gone to Mum.'

Will laughed at this. It wasn't vindictive, but the idea that their mother would be able to help was so ludicrous. His sister may not have wanted the guilt, but she wasn't averse to piling it onto him.

'No, you wouldn't, because she couldn't bail you out of this even if she wanted to.' He walked up to Ren and lifted her chin up with his hand. 'And I never said I wouldn't help, but six hundred is a lot to ask for,' he said, his tone finally softening. There was a look in her eyes that he didn't like, a look that was past anger, verging on the side of helplessness. 'Lawrencia, you need to tell me what's going on.'

She looked at him like he'd slapped her, and suddenly her body sagged as if she were a balloon and all the air had abruptly been sucked out of it.

'I'm sorry, but...' She stepped back. 'This is different, the people Jimmy has got involved with...'

He knew it, despite all her protests he had seen where this was going. But right now an 'I told you so' wasn't going to help. He shook his head sadly, wondering how his sister had got into such a stupid situation. He took her hand in his and guided her to the little wall, where they both sat.

'Listen, I'm going away for the weekend, but when I come back we'll talk.' Will breathed deeply, feeling all kinds of emotions welling up inside. 'I think a proper talk is long overdue, don't you?'

'Yes.' Ren sniffed, no longer trying to hold back the tears. 'Billy... Will, I'm in so much trouble.'

Without meaning to, Will found himself holding his sister in a strong embrace. He squeezed tightly, thinking he saw something of his kid sister returning at last. 'We'll talk. While I'm away I want you to stay here, with Curtis.'

'What about Jimmy?'

'What about him? Jake will be on hand, if Jimmy kicks off just give Jake a bell. He doesn't live far.' He pulled back and held her by the shoulders. 'Do you understand? This has to end now. Curtis has to be your priority.'

Ren nodded, although Will could still see the doubt in her eyes. But there was little else he could do. He glanced at his watch. He had forty minutes to get to Fenchurch Street, and since the car was still at the garage he'd need every one of those forty minutes.

'I need to get going, but you're going to stay here, right?'

'Of course, what else can I do?' Ren reached forward and hugged him again. 'I love you, Billy, you know that?'

For the first time in ages Will did know, but the amount of gratitude in his sister's voice worried him. There would be so much to do when he got back, both in his personal life and at work. He wasn't sure he was looking forward to it, but he now knew that there were things he could no longer run from. He pulled himself from his sister and stood, knowing he ought to tell her how much he loved her, but somehow he just couldn't find the words.

'Come on,' he said instead. 'Go and see your son. I'll explain things to Jake.'

He waited for her to stand, and the two of them entered the house. As they did, Ren said, 'Loving the new look, by the way, it's very you.'

*

Jake stood at the door and watched his old friend walk towards the Broadway. He didn't understand it, but Jake couldn't help escape the feeling that his old friend was never going to return.

He glanced back at Lawrencia, who was standing behind him holding Curtis. He'd have to give Amy a ring and tell her how their plans had been scuppered. Sticking around to keep an eye on Lawrencia was going to make for a long weekend. He just hoped Jimmy did try to kick off; he needed to vent somewhere.

*

'Yeah, I'm just down the road from his house. He's outside saying goodbye to Jake.'

Looking out across the Thames Estuary, Frederick smiled at the news. He had planned for this for so long now, and finally the moment was almost here.

'You have done well, Stephen.'

'Have I ever let you down?'

'No, you haven't, that much is true. But then you wouldn't, not unless you want your supply of Red Source to dry up.'

'Ah, man, you got me there. The stuff Anna provided is good shit.'

'The best, Stephen, the best.'

'Yeah, but not as good as yours. Don't get me wrong, man, I'm not complaining, but yours was the best.'

'You have no idea,' Frederick said, tiring of the banter.

'Is this enough to get me an audience with the Three then?'

Frederick grinned. 'One step closer.'

'Okay.' There was now a trace of uncertainty in Stephen's voice. 'Will I be able to get some of your Red soon?'

'Of course.'

'Sweet. Um, okay then, bye, Robin.'

Frederick ended the call, and smiled softly, imagining Will on his journey. 'So much for Charlie,' he said, and set off along the esplanade towards Southend Central.

8. What Happened to Robin Turner

His work for the Three done, Frederick made his way slowly up Hawthorn Road. He didn't mind Ashington too much, a largely urban town in the north east of England. He'd been sent to worse places in the centuries he'd served as the Three's special envoy, and Ashington was... nice. He'd rather be in London, keeping an eye on Willem Townsend, but he had duties that did not allow him the luxury of such excesses. He had spent far too much time in London in the last few months, anyway, ever since he'd first spotted Willem outside that café, and Lady Isobel was beginning to get a little curious. If he continued it would only be a matter of time before Celeste found out, and he wasn't ready to share yet.

He needed to be absolutely sure first. If what the Book said was true, then a few more years had to pass before he could make his move, enough time for him to be certain of the ka he'd sensed when he stumbled into Willem.

It was *him*, Frederick was so sure, but not absolutely. A few other things needed clarity first.

That was why he now walked up Hawthorn Road, following the teen before him. Eight decades had passed by so quickly, and now, once again, it was time.

He'd been following Robin Turner for a few days now, delving into the human's mind. Such a fragile thing, even the weakest mind trawler would have had no difficulty reading the surface thoughts of Robin. Frederick had learned what he needed, and knew that after work Robin always popped by his mother's before going on to his girlfriend's flat. And he knew that the path he took was always the same.

On cue, Robin turned into Hirst Park, and Frederick quickened his pace. Robin reminded him of so many others he'd known over the years. Dead on six feet tall, thin but not slim, with dark hair and deep brown eyes. Just like with all the others, Robin had the kind of eyes that sucked a person right in.

How could Frederick resist? *Especially* now.

He turned into Hirst Park himself, and was surprised to see Robin standing there, his body tense, fists clenched. As Frederick had suspected, Robin knew he was being followed. Which is what Frederick liked; he never picked the weak ones. There was no fun in that at all.

'What the fuck, man! What are you, some kind of nonce?'

Frederick grinned, and shook his head. 'No, children have no interest for me. Younger than nineteen and...'

'You're sick!' Robin stepped forward. 'You've picked the wrong fucking man to stalk.'

'No, you're perfect.' Without warning, and faster than Robin could take another step, Frederick was right in Robin's face, one hand clamped around his throat. 'To be nineteen again,' Frederick whispered, and forced his mouth over Robin's.

*

The next morning a body was found in Hirst Park; the body of an old man. Desiccated and pale. And next to it, yet to be fully dried by the morning sun, blood. It was later reckoned to be almost eight pints in total, the amount to be found in an average sized man. Word spread quickly, and the press soon dubbed it the Ashington Hallowe'en Murder, even though the murder, if there was indeed one, occurred at the very least two days before Hallowe'en.

It was a mystery to the local police; even the best CID had to offer were stumped. Later forensic reports shed little light; just added to the mystery. The corpse was empty of all but a miniscule amount of blood. That blood was compared to the excess found on the path, but the tests came back negative. Whoever the eight pints belonged to, it was not the old man.

A couple of days into the investigation, a specialist was called in from London. Detective Sergeant Alyson Rowe had a nose for unusual forensic cases. She was in her late twenties, a large woman in every way, and she had a reputation for her stubbornness. Once she got her teeth into a puzzle she would not relent until she uncovered the truth. She was what her superiors called unconventional, but nonetheless her instincts and ability were trusted. Word had it that she would make detective chief inspector within five years.

Even she was puzzled by this one, though, not that she was ready to be beaten. It was just the kind of challenge she enjoyed.

One body emptied of its blood (the press said *drained*, but no exit wound had been found, besides which Rowe did not like the implications the word *drained* brought with it), found next to enough blood to fill a body. Yet the blood clearly did not come from the empty body. It was grizzly, but an unexpected link to the crime soon revealed itself when DS Rowe happened across a missing person's report, filed by a Mrs Ann-Mari Turner. Her son, Robin, had never returned home on the night of October 28th. It was his custom, after work, to pop in to visit his mother before returning home to his girlfriend, but that night he did not return. The route he took was always a short-cut through Hirst Park.

Rowe had a hunch, a macabre hunch to be sure, but a hunch nonetheless. Her superiors did not like it, but they trusted her instincts enough to allow her to obtain a DNA sample off Robin's mother. It took some time, but after two weeks the DNA comparison came back with the most gruesome results. The eight pints of blood belonged to Robin Turner.

Detective Chief Inspector Russell did not like this new dimension to the investigation. How could they explain this to Robin's family? Rowe's suggestion was to not tell them; let them think that Robin was simply missing, that they would continue to investigate *that*. Russell was concerned, so he sent Rowe's immediate superior to Ashington to talk to her.

'We're not liking this, Aly,' Detective Inspector Carbis said, 'are we?'

Rowe recognised the look in his dark eyes, but they had been friends since she joined the Force. He was responsible for her transfer to CID. He trusted her instincts as much as she did, and he knew that she'd walk down whatever path she had to in order to solve the mystery. She didn't care how dark a path it turned out to be.

'You haven't heard the worst of it yet, Gary,' she replied. This was, at least for now, still informal and off the record. They were meeting in a quiet corner of a pub near Hirst Park, Carbis drinking a bottle of Smirnoff Ice while Rowe downed a pint of lager. 'I managed to track down the identity of the old man. His name was Cliff Goleman, and he went missing in 1917! At the age of nineteen.'

'The same age as Robin.'

Rowe nodded slowly. 'You saw Goleman's body; did it look 104 years old to you?'

'I don't think I've seen a body that old, Aly, living or dead.'

At this Rowe smiled. 'Okay, fair point. But according to the autopsy, the heart, liver... all the internal organs are consistent with a man of no more than sixty years.'

'Then it can't be the same man. DNA records didn't even exist in... when did you say? 1917? This is insane, Aly. Insane.'

'I know.' Rowe grinned and finished the rest of her pint. 'The DNA results led me to Goleman's grandson. He's fifty-eight, by the way, and the spit of Cliff.'

Carbis shook his head. 'No, I'm not buying it. How could you even have found out about Goleman's disappearance? Our own record keeping was bad enough thirty years ago, let alone eighty-five years ago.'

'Harry Goleman is a lifer at the Scrubs, so his DNA is on the system. Seeing his picture was a bit of a shock, since for a moment I was sure I was looking at our corpse. A bit of research later and I'm reading about his grandfather going missing at nineteen, only three months after his marriage, leaving behind a wife who was, unknowingly at the time, two months pregnant. The gears shifted in my brain.'

Carbis narrowed his eyes. 'Knowing how your brain works, I'm not surprised.' For a moment he looked down at the bottle in his hand, while Rowe watched his rapidly thinning crown. 'What do you propose we do?'

'Let me continue to investigate this. A man presumed dead eight decades ago turns up, healthy as a sixty-year-old – well, other than the complete loss of blood – next to eight pints of blood that should, by rights, still be in Robin Turner's body, which is now missing.' She paused for a minute, before delivering her final card. 'We've not seen the last of Robin Turner.'

'This is quite a limb you're out on.'

'I know, but it's my limb. And I know I am right,' Rowe added with complete certainty.

*

DI Gary Carbis was late for work. He had foolishly agreed to keep an eye on his fourteen-year-old niece, while his brother and sister-in-law enjoyed a dirty anniversary weekend in the Cotswolds. He didn't quite understand why anyone would want to visit such a picturesque location and spend the entire weekend under the covers, but then, he supposed, if he was involved with someone he'd know. It was time to change that. He didn't want to pressure Aly, but he wasn't going to act like some damn teenager and worry about destroying their friendship, either. They were both adults, and they could handle the fallout.

He paused in the doorway of the lounge. He had merely intended to pop his head in and say goodbye to Beth, but his eyes were drawn to the image on the desktop monitor. Two men, arms over each other's shoulders, smiling at the camera, standing, unless Carbis was mistaken, in Canada Square.

'What's this?' he asked, walking up behind his niece.

Beth glanced behind her. 'A website about BASE jumping?' Gary winced at the way her answer was given as a question. It was an irritating thing that she had picked up of late – he blamed too much American TV. 'Doing research for a school project,' she added, her voice reeking with guilt.

Gary smiled. Clearly not school work. But it didn't matter; at least the guys were fully clothed. He leaned in closer to look at the caption beneath the picture. Steve Krueger and...

Before he was even out of the door, Gary had his mobile to his ear, and Aly on the other end. She barely had a chance to say hello before Gary said, 'I take it all back. You were spot on. Robin Turner has resurfaced.'

*

Rowe met with Carbis several hours after the interview with Stephen Krueger. She spent a little time driving around Hammersmith and Chiswick, gathering her thoughts before calling Carbis at the Yard. He agreed to meet her at *The Slug & Lettuce* just off Fulham Broadway. Over food and a drink (non-alcoholic for a change), she told him everything she had learned from Krueger – which was, mostly, not a lot.

'Do you believe him?' Gary asked.

It was funny, whenever she saw him at work she thought of him as Carbis, much like all her colleagues did, but outside of the Yard she always thought of him by his first name. Outside the grey walls of Scotland Yard they were friends, regardless of their conversation, but inside he was her boss. Now he was her friend again.

'I believe he's telling the truth about how they met, and maybe even that they only see each other occasionally. But, no, I don't believe that Krueger doesn't know where Turner lives. Also...' Rowe paused. It shouldn't make a difference to her, after all she barely knew the Turner family, but she felt betrayed by what she had discovered. 'I *believe* that Krueger and Turner have a... physical relationship.'

'I thought Turner had a girlfriend in Ashington?'

'One he hasn't been in contact with for over five months?' Rowe shrugged. 'There's a lot going on here I don't understand. Every drop of his blood was left in Hirst Park, and yet he's in London, alive and well and involved in extreme sports and, I'm convinced, a sexual relationship with another man.'

'Did DC Swanson agree with that?'

Rowe pulled back sharply. Gary never called into question her hunches before, and had certainly never compared her opinion to that of a relatively new transfer to CID. Rochelle Swanson had accompanied her to interview Krueger; it would have looked strange had Rowe gone on her own, so it made sense to take someone who had only been out of uniform for a week. An officer who would never question anything her sergeant said.

'Of course she did, Gary, I've been a sergeant in the Met for a year now, she'll agree that red is green if I told her to.'

Gary shook his head and laughed. 'Don't be so sure, Aly. Swanson is one to watch out for. An asset to the team.'

Rowe raised an eyebrow. 'You saying I got competition?'

'Sure, I reckon she'll keep you on your toes.'

For a moment Rowe said nothing. If Gary thought that, then she would keep an eye on Swanson. Another ally in the Force could only be a good thing. 'Okay, fine, so anyway, back to my point. There is much that is wrong with Robin Turner even being alive, let alone in a relationship with a man.'

Gary sipped his water. 'This is a weird case, even by your standards, Aly.'

'It is.' Rowe narrowed her eyes in thought. 'I will get to the bottom of it. Krueger is my only lead right now, but if I can get to talk to Robin Turner... He has to know what happened in Hirst Park.'

'Do you think Krueger will contact you?'

Rowe hoped so. She had left her contact details with Krueger, told him that Turner had family in Ashington who were worried about him. Including a girlfriend. This little fact bothered Krueger, as much as he had tried to hide it. She knew body language, and she knew the look of jealousy. Krueger clearly did not know Turner as well as he thought. It was the only leverage she had right now and she drove that fact home before she left Krueger's flat on Clem Atlee Estate. Would he contact her?

'Depends on what happens when they next meet. How honest Turner is with him. Krueger's a driven man, a store manager at only twenty-two, he's not the type to let sleeping dogs lie.' She shook her head. 'No, he won't let this drop. He'll want to know everything about Turner. If he doesn't like what he hears, he'll call.'

'And if he doesn't?'

At this Rowe smiled. 'We keep an eye on him.'

'Yes, and despite the restrictions on budget and manpower, you'll pull every string you can to get your own way.'

'You know me so well, Gary.'

Gary grinned at her. 'Yes, I know. Which is why it's about time we went on a date.'

Rowe wasn't sure what kind of reaction Gary expected, but she could tell she caught him off guard with her laugh. 'Took you long enough to ask,' she said with a wink.

*

It wasn't the first time the police had become peripherally aware of his people, and it wouldn't be the last. There were procedures in place to remove such interest, and normally Frederick would have made a few calls to start such procedures. But this time he was working under the radar of the upiór world. None could know of his contact with Stephen, not until he was sure about Willem Townsend.

'You never told me about your girlfriend, Robin,' Stephen said.

Humans were so parochial and singular. Frederick forgot how irritating they could be. 'Stephen, never mind what DS Rowe told you. You've had a *taste* of my life, you know it's much bigger than a single relationship.'

'Bigger than you and me?'

'Bigger than anything you've ever experienced. You must trust me, Stephen.'

'I want to,' Stephen began, but his voice faltered.

It was clear by his tone that he really meant that, but as ever, dipping a toe into the dangerous waters of the upiór world caused another human to pause. He had seen it happen many times. Some upiór believed their people needed humans, to keep them connected to the world. As powerful as they were, they needed to use the human world, to shroud themselves among every day events. And there was always one way to hook a human in.

'I know you do. I will need to go away for a while, give this Rowe a chance to get tired of pursuing me. But I will be back.'

'Where will you go? What about me?'

Frederick smiled. 'Continue about your business, act as if there is nothing amiss. I will put you in contact with someone who will keep you in Red Source; it will not be as powerful as that which you have already experienced, but it will provide you with the high you need.'

'Dude, I don't know, this is all...'

'Stephen, trust me. I chose you for a reason. We are at the start of a very long journey; you stand on the edge of an existence unlike anything you can even contemplate. I will continue to guide you, but you must trust me.'

For a moment there was silence on the other end of the line, then Stephen said, 'okay.'

It was time to return to France. Celeste would, of course, be pleased to see him, as would Theodor. He could probably do without the irritation of Eryn, but if nothing else Eryn would provide him with a useful distraction while he waited for DS Rowe's interest to die down. And in the meantime, he could advise Stephen from afar, continue to play his role as Robin, watching over Stephen as Stephen watched over Willem.

There were still eight years until Willem needed to be in Southend, eight years until it was time for the prophecy to be fulfilled.

That gave Frederick plenty of time to plan, to manoeuvre Willem into position.

9. The Wrong Man

It had taken Frederick seven years before he returned to England, in the meantime he had continued to study the Book, to learn all that he could learn, prepare him for this day. And now, after several months of living in Southend, of watching things fall into place – Willem's falling for Charlie, a man living in Southend, and Frederick using his Robin identity to carefully push Willem into meeting Charlie this weekend, and more, including ensuring that the Three were at the Residence... Now, it was time.

As the train pulled into Upminster Station, Frederick looked up from his paper. He hadn't been waiting too long, probably about fifteen minutes, but he was getting impatient. Although it had only been less than a decade since that fateful day outside the cafe in Newington Green, and a decade was no time at all for someone as long lived as he, Frederick had been waiting a lot longer than that.

Careful to not draw attention, Frederick casually stood and discarded the newspaper on the bench. It seemed a common enough thing to do, as he often came across abandoned papers on stations and trains. He watched the carriages move by. The train slowed, and he smiled.

Yes, Will was indeed on that train. Already he had passed by, but that was fine. Frederick wanted to prepare himself.

As he stepped onto the train he laughed. Prepare himself! Over 222 years; wasn't that enough time to prepare for this moment?

Frederick continued smiling as he started up the carriage. He reached out his subconscious, keeping the conscious part of his mind on his path through the carriages. Even now he could feel Will, completely unaware of the mental violation, his mind full of insular hopes about what the weekend for him and Charlie would bring. Such a parochial expectation. It amazed Frederick how little Will was aware of his own potential.

Frederick's people had a gift that allowed them to sense another of their kind, an awareness of the ka within. Such a gift that it mattered little if they'd previously met, they just knew they were of the same people before they even laid eyes on the other. It was that sense that Frederick had got in 2002 when he had quite literally bumped into Will during a visit to London. And as he had sat in the cafe, observing Will, he had been reminded of that verse from the Book.

Onuris shall appear unto the one who sees, shrouded in the shell of a mortal man, and with him shall return hope. But before he is known pain will rage in him; he shall be rejected by his past and the fires of truth will explode in the hunger.

He wished Melinda the Scribe was still with them, but she had met an unfortunate end many years before Newington Green, and Frederick's brief encounter with Will. She had shown him how to translate the Book, as Wamukota had promised, and had been sworn to secrecy over it, but the Brotherhood had learned of her. Removing her before they got to her was the only thing the Three could do; a fact that Frederick still held against them.

Even without Melinda's amazing linguistic skills, it became clear to Frederick that Will was the one the Book promised, a human carrying the dormant ka of the oldest of Frederick's people. There was no other explanation for the sense Frederick had got when he was close to Will.

Frederick dared not go too close to Will, for fear of messing up; everything was preordained and had to happen at given times. But now he could feel Will's mind once again, sense the purity in him, untouched and unknown for hundreds of years.

Frederick was not as adept at mind trawling as Celeste, but even with his limited abilities he could feel many closed doors in Will's mind.

He had, of course, told the Three, but they were more cautious. Even Celeste, who trusted Frederick so much, paused and warned Frederick not to get too caught up in this human. They had all heard stories of those of their people who had become so enamoured with certain humans that they projected ka echoes on their objects of interest, convincing themselves that they had met another of their kind. Celeste was not saying this was the case with Will, but until the Three were able to meet him themselves, they were unwilling to commit their resources to awakening that old soul in Will, if indeed he possessed one.

On one level Frederick understood their caution, and agreed it was necessary, but he *knew* he was right about this. And by the end of the day, the Three would also know.

Frederick stopped walking for a moment. Will was aware of him, like an itch that couldn't quite be found. Frederick smiled, pleasantly surprised by this. If further proof was required, this was it; only one of his people would be able to feel such a probing of the thoughts.

Frederick carried on into the next carriage, his unconscious mind trying to dig just that bit deeper. It was to no avail; the doors were firmly shut.

No matter. He had reached Will.

'Excuse me?'

Will almost jumped.

Frederick smiled down at him. 'Is this seat free?' he asked, indicating the aisle seat that had a rucksack sitting on it.

At first Will glanced around at all the other empty seats, but when he returned his look to Frederick he was met with the most suggestive smile Frederick could offer. Will smiled, blushing.

'Oh, sure. Yeah, of course. Sorry.' Will lifted his rucksack and tried to shove it on the floor space between his legs.

Frederick sat down while Will continued to struggle, their legs now touching. Will noticed and attempted to shift over a little, mumbling another apology.

'Not to worry,' Frederick said.

For a while they sat in silence, Will looking out of the window while Frederick sat back in his seat and closed his eyes. He placed one hand on his left leg, his fingers gently brushing against Will's right leg, while his other hand rested on the belt of his jeans, his thumb gently rubbing his abdomen beneath his purple silk shirt. A slight shifting of the leg told Frederick that Will had moved and was now no doubt snatching quick glances at Frederick's right hand, the index finger of which was now playing with the gap between the buttons, offering a tantalising glimpse of his muscled physique beneath.

He smiled and opened one eye, just in time to catch Will looking. Will noticed but found he couldn't pull his eyes away from Frederick.

As Stephen had said, Will liked the younger men, and Frederick certainly seemed to fit the bill there. On the surface he was twenty-seven, but thanks to his preternatural life force he looked a few years younger, even though neither was actually true. He had over two centuries on Will.

'Have to be honest here,' Frederick said, still bearing the smile that held Will captive, 'I spotted you as the train pulled into Upminster, and I just knew I had to come and sit next to you.'

Will swallowed. 'Why?' he asked, his voice quivering with nerves, even though his eyes were now smiling.

'I think you know why,' Frederick pointed out, removing his hand from his shirt. 'Someone as good looking as you shouldn't be travelling alone.'

'What makes you think I'm alone?'

Frederick looked around at the people who were studiously ignoring the two men who seemed to be in the middle of something very private. That was one of the things that he loved about humans, their capacity for denial was so great it was almost astounding.

'Doesn't appear to be anyone else with you.'

'Okay, good point, but I might be meeting someone when I get off.'

Frederick smiled again. 'True. Where you heading?'

'Southend.'

'Me too. Looks like we'll be getting off together then.'

Will tried to not smile, and Frederick gave him props for that, but it was clear that he was very interested now.

*

'What a dump,' said the boy, as the three of them exited Southend Central Railway Station.

The old man with him smiled, and looked at the girl. 'Your brother is such an optimist.' He sniffed, and ran a hand over his thick white beard. 'Air is certainly fresher than London.'

'That's not difficult,' the girl said. 'But we're not tourists, who cares what the weather is like.'

'No, but we do have some, ah, free time, isn't that what you kids call it?'

'I haven't been a kid for a long time.'

'Yes, well, I suppose you are almost twenty now.'

'That's not what I meant.'

The old man smiled. 'Oh, I know, Maia. You've had a hard life. Well, soon be time to start putting things in order again.'

'Never liked it here,' the boy continued, as if the other two hadn't said anything. 'Mum used to bring us here when we were kids.'

The girl scowled. Talking about their mum was one thing she had no intention of doing. Not right now, not while they were on mission.

She closed her eyes. 'They're here,' she said. 'I can feel them.'

'Yes, plenty of them,' the old man said. 'Drawn to the presence of the Three. Good, just as we'd hoped. Come, let us find some accommodation. We have much to do before tomorrow night.'

And so saying, the old man set off, pulling his suitcase behind him. Maia looked at her brother, who as ever spent most of his time looking at the floor, sullen and withdrawn.

'Come on, Dar, it'll be over soon.'

'I wish,' he said, and stalked off, following Edward Lomax.

*

Jake looked up at the clock.

'Stop worrying,' Amy said from her position on the couch, her head resting on his chest. 'He'll be fine.'

'He's about halfway there.'

'I don't know who's more nervous, you or him.'

'I know, it's just...' Jake shrugged, feeling foolish.

'You're worried, I get it, but you shouldn't be. He's a grown man.'

'Yeah, but he's not the kind of man to do something like this.'

'Which means it's about time he did. Which reminds me.' Amy moved herself into a sitting position. 'About time the little man was up from his nap, yeah?'

'Yeah,' Jake said, lifting himself off the couch. 'And about time Lawrencia was back too.'

'You can't be her keeper, Jacob. You're not Will. As long as Curtis is safe.'

Jake stopped in the doorway and just looked at Amy. He smiled, knowing just how lucky he was to have her. Not only in general, but right at that moment. She had agreed to leave work early as soon as she had learned Jake's promise to keep an eye on Curtis and Lawrencia until Sunday. As soon as she had turned up at Will's, Lawrencia had left without barely a hello to Amy. Jake didn't mind. He kind of enjoyed the idea of it just being him, Amy and Curtis.

'Go on, I'll still be here when you get back,' Amy said, shaking her head. 'I'll even put the kettle on for you.' She too got up, walked over to the doorway, gave him a peck on the cheek and continued on to the kitchen.

Jake watched her, his eyes lingering on her ample behind. It made a comfortable pillow he thought and shook his head clear of such thoughts. Now wasn't the time, not with a child about to be bouncing about the place.

He rushed up the stairs and stopped at the bottom of the second flight, which led into Will's attic bedroom. He frowned, a feeling of dread creeping through him.

He swallowed, put on a smile and opened the door to Curtis' room, to find the little boy running around like a nutter, his arms out wide, laughing.

'What are you doing?' Jake said, trying not to laugh.

'I'm flying!'

'Bet you can fly higher than that.'

Jake scooped him up in his arms and flew him all the way downstairs, and for a short while, Curtis' laughter filling the house, Jake didn't have a care in his heart.

*

Will was, in part, being seduced and, in part, manipulated but Frederick had no problem with that. Despite all the literature and films that implied otherwise, his people had no way to beguile humans. And thus, it was necessary to employ all the tricks they had learned; firstly in their own lives as humans, and secondly in their much longer lives after the First Death.

Frederick had learned much in his time about how to get what he wanted, through both nefarious means and other more honest ones. Either did not bother him so much.

After almost 290 years since his Rebirth, he had learned a different code of conduct and the strictures of human morality rarely came into it. So it was with Will. To get him where Frederick needed him, he would happily employ whatever tactic he needed.

Sexual persuasion was a tried and tested method. Humanity was a beast enslaved by sexual appetite, thusly such a tool of manipulation was most often called upon when his people needed something from any given human. With Will it was probably the best weapon Frederick had; he had studied Will's life in depth and he knew that this was a man with much sexual tension about him. So tightly wound up by his work responsibilities and the extra pressures piled onto him by his sister and mother, that he had little chance for sexual release.

As much as Will liked to think he was interested primarily in the emotional and intellectual bond he'd felt with Charlie, Frederick knew better. The need for sex drove Will into Charlie's arms most of all. And if Will believed Charlie offered release, his mind would boggle at what Frederick offered.

Already, in the hour-long journey from Upminster, Will was getting a hint of bigger things. A passionate kiss in the carriage toilets was just a taste of what Frederick promised later. If Will wanted to step out of his box, Frederick was the means by which he could not only step, but jump.

'Your sister does sound like a pain,' Frederick was saying as they passed through the ticket barriers at Southend Central. Sexual release was a great driving force, but another thing that humans sought was a kindred spirit. A person of like-mind who understood them. That, at least, was one thing Frederick's own people shared with humanity.

'Ah, you have no idea.' Will stopped once outside, looking around, the infamous stranger in a strange land. He held his holdall in one hand, while his rucksack was slung over the other shoulder. Among the crowd of people milling about he stuck out like a sore thumb, yet another holidaymaker who had come to Southend to enjoy the beach and spend much money in the arcades that littered the seafront. He glanced at his watch.

'Late for something?' Frederick asked innocently.

'Nah, early actually. Supposed to be meeting someone at half one.'

'Oh yes, you said. Well, maybe a decent coffee is needed while you wait.' Frederick smiled. 'If you're going to leave me for someone else then I might as well enjoy the time I have with you.'

He was pleased at how quickly Will decided that a coffee would be a good idea, but not as pleased as he was by the look of disappointment on Will's face when he realised that they'd soon be parting company.

They walked down the slope and came out on the high street where Frederick led Will to the closest Starbuck's. Once inside, Frederick suggested a table near to the counter. Will placed his bags on the floor and sat down, facing the windows to watch out for Charlie. His tone confirmed his disappointment at the prospect.

'I'll get the coffees in,' Frederick said.

'Fred, you don't have to.'

'No, but I want to.' Frederick smiled, and placed a kiss on Will's lips. Will did not pull away and, when Frederick stood up, Will's eyes were still closed, savouring the taste of the lips on his. He opened his eyes slowly, his face lighting up with a broad grin. Frederick winked at him. 'Won't be long.'

While he approached the counter and ordered the two cappuccinos, he continued to probe Will's thoughts. A task he was finding increasingly difficult. At first it had been simplicity itself, but now he could barely read Will's surface thoughts.

Frederick ordered the drinks and looked over at Will, who was now looking out of the window, his hands playing with the phone in his jeans' pocket. He took the drinks off the girl behind the espresso machine and returned to the table. Will removed his hand from his pocket and smiled at Frederick.

'This better be good coffee,' Will said, accepting the long cup. 'I'm not a huge fan of Starbuck's, what with them being the competition.'

'The competition?' Frederick asked, taking his seat once again, then nodded as if he'd only just remembered. 'Of course, your expanding empire. Do you think you will get that unit at King's Cross?'

'Don't see why not. And if I do... well, I'll be shipping Steve there.'

'Steve?'

'The best manager I got. He's worked for me for so long now, most reliable and trustworthy guy I've ever known,' Will said, and Frederick nodded in understanding.

'Always good to have reliable people around you. People you can trust.'

'For sure. So, yeah, Steve will set up the new place without breaking a stride, then time to make him area manager. I'll be needing one by then. Besides, he's kind of acting like one at the moment anyway, since he's basically running both the North End Road and High Street Ken shops.'

'Ah,' was all Frederick said to that, and watched Will sip the hot contents of his cup.

It was then that Frederick decided that when Will was in touch with his true self he would take great pleasure in telling Will about Stephen's betrayal. It would be interesting to see how the new and improved Will would deal with Stephen.

'Cappuccino up to standard?'

'Yes,' Will said, smiling with his brown eyes, 'it'll pass muster.'

'Glad to hear it,' Frederick said with a laugh. They sat there in silence for a moment, just looking at each other, the activities of the coffee shop fading away into the background. Right then nothing else seemed to matter.

Frederick sat forward and took Will's hands in his, glad to see that he did not pull back. 'We're connecting, are we not?'

Will swallowed slowly, and nodded his head. 'Yes,' he answered in a low voice. 'I've no idea why, but I can't help but feel this was meant to be.' He laughed, and shook his head. 'Sorry. How cheesy was that?'

'Not the bit of it.'

Almost as if some force was pulling them together, they both leaned forward and their lips met. It was a kiss that put their brief encounter in the toilet on the train to shame, seeming to last forever. Eventually they drew their tongues back into their own mouths and sat back. Will went to speak, but no words came.

'Well,' Frederick began, but stopped when he noticed Will's attention focused on something just behind his shoulder.

Frederick turned slowly.

Standing in the doorway was Charlie.

Frederick wasn't sure what was cuter, Charlie's crumbling visage or the Clinton's bag he held in one hand, which no doubt contained some little gift for Will.

Frederick's lips curled up into a smile and he glanced at Will, not entirely surprised to see the guilt sweeping across his features.

'Will,' Charlie said, but only just.

Frederick didn't look to see, but it was clear that Charlie was sinking into a pit of confusion and hurt. He didn't much care, bigger things were playing out.

Instead, Frederick watched Will intently, enjoying the way the guilt slowly transformed into determination when his eyes locked with Frederick's.

Will had made up his mind.

Frederick looked back at Charlie, smiling at the human who had lost the man he had hoped to love. The meaning behind Frederick's smile was clear.

You have lost, Charlie, Will is mine. Now go, before I eviscerate you.

It seemed unlikely his thoughts penetrated Charlie's mind, but the human got the message, turned and left.

'So, that was...?' Frederick asked, returning his attention to Will, smile and voice the epitome of innocence.

'Doesn't matter,' Will replied, looking at the cappuccino in his hands. He shook his head. 'It's strange. I came here to be with Charlie, but now...' He lifted his head, and Frederick was rewarded by a sparkle in his brown eyes. 'All that matters, is right now. You and I.'

As it should be, Frederick thought.

10. A Meeting with Three

It was decided quickly that Will would accompany Frederick while he met up with his 'business partners', before they headed back to Frederick's place to get changed for a night out. They backtracked to the train station and got a train to Benfleet, and from there a bus onto Canvey Island.

As usual Frederick felt his blood warm at the thought of a reunion with Celeste. It wasn't like he hadn't seen her for a long time; two days was a short time in anyone's life, especially his. But time apart from Celeste was never a good thing really, often necessary, but rarely out of choice. They had been together for so long it was almost as if they lost something of their functionality when away from each other. But on occasion, parting company was needed and the last two days was a case in point.

Will stopped outside the Residence and looked up at its imposing edifice. He glanced at Frederick.

'I'll wait out here.'

'Why?'

Will frowned, unable to take his eyes off the grey building. 'I don't know, I just...' He shook his head and turned to Frederick, his face conveying his helplessness in expressing his feelings on this. He forced a smile. 'Just being silly, probably. But I don't want to get in your way. I'll wait here while you take care of your business.'

A smokescreen, and Frederick knew it. The ka in him was at odds now, and his humanity was fighting against it. Frederick smiled to himself and placed an arm around Will's shoulders.

'It is going to be fine. I told them I've got company, and they're looking forward to meeting you.'

'Yeah?'

'For sure.'

Frederick watched Will's face as the man weighed it up. He felt Will relax under his arm.

'Okay, cool,' Will said with a firm nod.

'Good.' Frederick hefted the weight of Will's holdall in his hand and took Will's hand in his free one. He gave it a gentle squeeze. 'Come on, then.'

Hand in hand they walked towards the Residence. As its shadow blocked out the sun, Will removed his glasses. Frederick preferred him without them; he liked being able to see Will's mortal eyes. The natural colour still in them.

'When did you tell your associates you had company?' Will asked suddenly, as Frederick released his hand and reached for the door.

'Ah.'

*

They walked through a high vaulted passageway that ran the length of the Residence, having left Will's luggage in a small room at the front of the building. The passage split the Residence in two, with doors along either wall leading to various rooms and chambers. In the centre of the ceiling high above was a large skylight, the sun shining through. Frederick noted how Will kept his hand up, to protect his eyes from the light. Occasional balconies ran the length of the passageway, with three of them branching out to bridges linking several of the upper chambers. There were no electric lights along the passage, instead torches made of kindling hung next to each of the paintings that filled the gaps between the doors all along the passage. The paintings were portraits of people known to Frederick; some more so than others, while a few of the paintings showed landscapes of places that he and Celeste had visited over their long years of companionship. Most of them sparked memories in him.

Over there was Strathclyde Loch in Scotland as it looked at the turn of the twentieth century, over here was a portrait of an elderly man in the tuxedo of a bygone era, his deep brown eyes watching as Will and Frederick passed by. Frederick smiled, he had always liked that old face; there was an air of wisdom about it that he missed greatly. Every time he saw the painting he felt wistful.

'That's you, isn't it?' Will asked.

For a second Frederick started in surprise, then realised Will was pointing at a different painting.

'Yes, that is indeed me.'

Of all the paintings in the passageway it was the only one not painted by Celeste. It showed Frederick and an old woman of about eighty, standing tall, her eyes still sparkling with strength despite her apparent age. They stood against the backdrop of *Château de Maupassant* in Marseilles, France. He reached out a hand and ran his fingers along the body of the woman.

'Your mother?'

Frederick shook his head and laughed. 'No, it's Ce...' He stopped himself abruptly. Some truths Will simply wasn't ready for. By the start of next week, though, so much would become clear to him. But not right now, so instead Frederick said, 'Someone very dear to me. It was painted about five years ago.'

'What happened to her? Is she...?'

Frederick placed an arm around Will's shoulder. 'She's still around. You will get to meet her soon.'

'Good,' Will said, allowing himself to be guided to a door a little further up the passage. 'I want to meet all the important people in your life, hear the stories they have about you. Learn about the person you were before meeting me.'

Frederick smiled, wishing he could say the same. He knew ample about the person Will was, but it was the person he was to become that interested Frederick mostly.

'More cheese?' he asked playfully.

Will laughed, looking away in embarrassment. 'A little.'

'Will, let's not rush things too much. We have all the time in the world, and much more besides.'

'Wait,' Will said, placing a hand over Frederick's to stop him opening the door.

Frederick looked at him closely, and was surprised to see something like fear in Will's eyes.

'Are you sure this is okay?'

'What do you mean?' Frederick asked, enjoying the feeling of warmth from Will's hand.

'I don't know. I just feel like I'm... intruding or something. I know you said these are your business partners, but...' He indicated the paintings. 'There's something more than just business here, Fred.'

He was clearly in two minds, which made a lot of sense. But Celeste was waiting to meet him, and Frederick couldn't keep her waiting for much longer. He released the door handle and linked his fingers with Will's, pulling him closer.

'Do you trust me?' he asked softly, their noses almost touching.

Will swallowed, but didn't answer.

'My business partners are the only family I've got left, Will. Understand that. We've worked together a very long time, we know each other intimately. I assure you that they will like you and can't wait to meet you.'

Will frowned. 'Yeah, you never answered that, either. How can they be exp—'

Frederick cut him off by placing his lips against Will's. The younger man quickly reciprocated. After a few moments Frederick pulled away, smiling.

'As we said, there's this connection between us, right?'

Will nodded.

'Okay, then trust me on this. Everything is going to be fine.'

Still holding Will's hand, Frederick turned and opened the door. Together they walked into the chamber beyond.

*

Jake stared at his phone. The message made no sense.

Arrived in Southend. All is good. Speak soon.

It was so impersonal, so not Will. Jake had been expecting something at some point, but not this. Not a text that told him nothing at all. All is good? What did that even mean?

'Bloody hell, Jacob, calm down. It means all is good,' Amy told him after he had rushed out into the back yard to show her the text.

'But it doesn't mean that. I mean, he should have texted ages ago. He was due in Southend around one, it's now almost three.'

'So, maybe he's just enjoying being away from his life? Enjoying being with Charlie.'

'I...'

Jake was reminded of their discussion during the all-nighter, about relationships and how it meant certain changes. Only... This was the first time Will had been with Charlie. Talking on the internet, a few Skype calls, surely that didn't class as a relationship...?

'Way I see it is this,' Amy said, taking the phone off Jake and closing the message. 'They've been involved almost half as long as we have; we've been able to see each other more or less when we want. And do we spend all our time worrying about our friends, thinking we need to update them on everything?'

'Well, of course not, we...'

She put a finger on his lips. 'Relax. If there's a problem, I'm sure Will will let us know, until them just let him have his time.'

'So don't respond?'

'No.' Amy handed his phone back to him. 'Let him have this.'

Jake took a deep breath. He was being an idiot, he could see that. Of course he was. He leaned forward and kissed Amy. 'What would I do without you?'

'Collapse into a puddle of sociopathy.'

Jake just smiled. He didn't even know what that meant.

*

Frederick felt odd going through the motions of decorum, but with Will accompanying him he had little choice. The 'newbie', to use the parlance of Will's generation, needed to understand and learn the rules of conduct when meeting with the Three. As soon as they were through the door, Frederick released Will's hand and offered him a reassuring smile.

The chamber was low lit, only a few candles providing the little illumination there was. It was very affected; everything in the chamber was designed to bring a sense of calm to those who wished to see the Three. To have them in the same place was a rare occurrence, and his people knew to appreciate the honour. Usually the Three remained separate of each other, but they all stood on the precipice of the greatest moment in their history and they needed to be together, to show a unified front in light of the great changes that were to come about with the arrival of the Seeker.

The walls had been stripped down to their bare bricks, with a massive intricately woven tapestry taking pride of place on the wall directly opposite the entrance. The tapestry showed an elegant female body, dressed in white, with the head of a lioness, on top of which sat the sun with a cobra wrapped around it. In one hand she held a sceptre, in the other an ankh – the key to the afterlife – dripping blood. This was the most important figure in the history of Frederick's people. It was placed to be the first thing people saw as they entered, to remind them of the truth that the Three represented. The rest of the chamber was spartan, the shadows from the candle flames dancing along the walls. It was merely an antechamber, a place for people to prepare for meeting the Three, and as such it didn't need extensive furnishings.

'Egyptian?' Will asked.

'Yes, the Goddess Sekhmet.' Frederick looked at Will, to see if there was any sign of recognition in his eyes as he walked over to the tapestry.

'What kind of work do you and your associates do? Another thing you've not told me,' Will added, looking away from the tapestry, clearly not realising the importance Sekhmet held for him.

'It's complicated,' Frederick said, not willing to say too much until he and the Three had a chance to confer, disturbed as he was by Will's lack of awareness. 'I will explain everything later, I promise.'

Thankfully, at that moment, the secondary door leading to the private room opened and out stepped Nate, Wa'eb to the Three. It was an old Egyptian term adopted hundreds of years ago by his people; originally it referred to an Egyptian priest, a pure one, who helped the high priests. But now it was a title given to the person who was, to all intents and purposes, little more than a glorified secretary. Nate was a diminutive and genial man, dressed as ever in a smart four-piece suit, complete with braided waistcoat. His transparent eyes regarded Will briefly, before he turned to Frederick.

He had the utmost respect for Frederick due to his unique standing with the Three, in particular with Celeste. Normally Frederick would not need to come before Nate first; he never needed an appointment to see Celeste. But, again, Will's presence changed that.

Frederick positioned himself so that Will could get a clear view of Nate and his eyes.

'Mr Holtzrichter, sir,' the Wa'eb began, hands held together. 'A pleasure to see you once again. How can I be of service?'

It was rare that Frederick was addressed by his family name, since it was never used in the human world and only a select few of his people knew of it. Like much of his past it remained shrouded, a secret known to only those Frederick trusted, the number of which he could count on one hand. Nate knew nothing of his past, but he knew the family name and Frederick appreciated the mark of respect given by its usage.

'You can inform the Three that I wish to speak to them.'

Frederick was mindful of Will's attention on him, the doubt clouding his face. He glanced at Will and offered a smile. Will frowned, this time not so easily buying the assurance, and looked at Nate. The Wa'eb was eyeing them, watching the exchange. He smiled and turned back to Frederick.

'Of course, sir.' Nate bowed and turned to the door.

Will sidled up to Frederick. 'His eyes,' he began, but before Frederick could respond, two people emerged from the room beyond.

As expected, the twins came out first. They weren't really twins, but for the longest time Eryn and Theodor had chosen twins as their vessels, an outward sign to all of their unbreakable bond.

Theodor, as was his wont when around humans, wore sunglasses to hide his translucent eyes; he didn't care much for the attentions of mortal men, drawn as they usually were by the blood that flowed behind his eyes. He stood to one side and allowed Eryn to view Will; she at least had the foresight to wear her blue contacts, which, unless Frederick was very much mistaken, were chosen specifically to match the electric blue hi-lites in her otherwise black hair. She stopped next to Theodor and leaned in closer to whisper something in his ear. So much for Eryn being considerate.

Frederick could feel Will looking at him, the doubt replaced by downright worry. Frederick took Will's hand in his, just as Celeste stepped into the chamber.

Radiant as ever, just by entering she made the chamber warmer, her presence filling up every spare bit of space. She was dressed in a flowing scarlet gown, which looked brilliant against her chocolate toned skin. With full lips she smiled at Frederick and opened her arms. They embraced, and she placed her mouth next to his ear.

'Are you still sure, *mon toujours?*'

'Yes,' Frederick said, equally as quiet, intoxicated by the delicate French cadence of her voice.

She released Frederick and crossed the chamber to Will. The twins watched her closely. Opening her arms, she said, 'Willem, *ma chére, c'est un grand plaisir de vous rencontrer enfin.*' She almost dragged him into her embrace, and it was quite obvious that Will was not very comfortable with this display of affection. Frederick couldn't help but grin largely.

'Will,' he said, 'allow me to introduce Celeste.'

Celeste let Will go and regarded him. He looked around.

'Erm,' he began, uncertainty etched in every line of his face. '*Bonjour?*'

Celeste smiled. 'Hello to you, too. It really is a pleasure to meet you, but if you'll excuse us. We need to speak to Frederick in private.' She looked around for Nate, who had sunk into the shadows when she entered the chamber.

He knew his place, and although he could not know it yet, he had just witnessed a turning point in history. Frederick wondered how many Nate would tell of this moment when the full truth was revealed to their people.

'Nate, please give Willem the guided tour. Treat him as an honoured guest, for that is what he is.'

'Of course,' Nate said, bowing his way out of the shadows. He walked over to the main door and opened it. 'This way, Mr Townsend.'

Will didn't move. Instead, he watched the Three return to their private room, then looked at Frederick enquiringly.

'How do they know my proper name? I haven't even told you tha—?'

Frederick took Will's hands in his. 'No questions yet; there will be plenty of time for answers later. Now I have business to which I must attend. Nate will take good care of you.'

Will opened his mouth to ask his question anyway, as Frederick knew he would, but Frederick placed a finger over his lips. 'Shh now. Later.'

Frederick stepped back and waited for Will to follow Nate. The man lingered for a moment longer and then, hesitantly, left the chamber. As he departed, Frederick tried to reach out his mind to Will, to get a sense of any new awareness he might have gained. But there was nothing, just the usual barely discernible surface thoughts.

*

'I still don't see why we all have to share a room,' Maia said.

'Isn't it obvious?' Lomax indicated Darrell, who was lying on the sofa of the double-bed hotel room. He was under a trance, oblivious to the tube that was in his arm and the blood that was being transferred into his body. Maia's blood.

'Not really. If you want to keep an eye on him, fine, but that doesn't mean you need to keep an eye on me, does it? He's back you know, Frederick. I can feel him nearby.'

Lomax joined Maia by the window. 'I know you are impatient, dear, but we're not here for Frederick. Not as such. We have spent months working on this, we don't rush it now.'

'Why not? I could just end it here.'

Lomax shook his head and put a hand on her shoulder. She tried to shrug him off, but his grip was like a vice. 'For many years, *many* years, I acted on impulse. I was a slave to my emotion, my need for vengeance. All I could think of was Theodor.'

'So what changed?'

'Perspective. Just like I changed yours. Although, it would appear, still not enough. Perhaps I need to remind you...?'

Maia closed her eyes, shut out the dark thoughts that Lomax's words brought to her mind. No, she couldn't go through all that again. She calmed her breathing.

'Fine. We'll wait. You can watch me too.'

'Excellent,' Lomax said, his tone now light again. He released her and crossed the hotel room. 'Don't worry, Maia, Darrell is primed. And tomorrow we can begin.'

Maia said nothing. She knew she was doing the right thing, the *only* thing. And she refused to listen to the small whisper of doubt in the corner of her mind.

*

'Him? There's no way that insipid fool is the one we've been waiting all this time for.'

Frederick closed the door behind him, not completely shocked to hear Eryn running her mouth as usual. Always the first to speak on any given subject, she tended to let her first thought be the crux of any discussion regardless of the evidence that might prove her wrong. Emotions ran high in Eryn, and still she had yet to learn to curb them. In truth Frederick suspected Eryn purposely refused to control them and considered them her greatest asset.

She pointed at Frederick, who merely looked at her in the most insouciant manner he could manage.

'It's quite obvious Freddy here has taken a shine to him,' Eryn said, the Welsh lilt to her voice just about clear. 'Classical case of ka transference here, that is.'

Frederick raised an eyebrow and sat down in the most ornate chair he could find, but said nothing. He grew tired of Eryn easily, and after so many years he was beyond rising to the bait of her calling him by anything but the name he had been given at his mortal birth.

Celeste moved over to him, and placed a hand on his shoulder. He looked up at her, and was rewarded by a smile of confidence.

'What do you think?' he asked her. 'With all due respect to Eryn, I somehow doubt her telepathic ability approaches yours, and is thus unqualified to make such a judgment.'

Eryn glared at him, but knew she couldn't argue that point. Celeste was, to their knowledge, the most accomplished mind trawler of their people. Theodor sat next to Eryn on the *chaise longue* and silently sipped the red liquid from his glass. Knowing Theodor, Frederick doubted it was wine. He removed his glasses and a look passed between the 'twins'. Eryn sat back to listen to what Celeste had to say.

'This Willem is something of a mystery. Trawling through a human mind is a delicate skill, one I have mastered over the years, but Willem is...' Celeste frowned, searching for the word. 'I don't know, but I cannot read his thoughts as clearly as I ought. There are doors closed in his mind, and behind those even more doors. It's like a maze hidden within a fortress, but I do not feel it's a wilful act on Willem's part. No, I think there is much about him that he has no notion of. But I get a sense of disjointed presence about him, almost like he's walking around in a suit that doesn't fit him.'

'Do you think he is the Seeker?' Frederick asked.

'I think it is a possibility.'

Eryn sat forward again. 'Then we need to arrange a test, to see if the truth emerges in the rage of hunger as the Book says.'

'Agreed,' Celeste and Frederick said in unison. Theodor merely nodded his silent agreement.

'But it has to be planned carefully,' Frederick continued.

'It will be brutal, *mon toujours*,' Celeste reminded him. 'It has to be.'

'I know, and if we are wrong then an innocent man could well be killed.'

'There is no such thing as innocence,' Eryn stated.

'Be that as it may, Eryn, my dear,' Celeste said, 'we do not wilfully kill humans unless absolutely necessary. Despite what the world may say of our ancestors, we are not monsters.' She looked down at Frederick. 'Where do you intend to take Willem, *mon toujours*?'

'Zinc, on Lucy Road. Gay nightclub seems the kind of thing he needs; one last chance to unwind.'

Eryn laughed. 'You see; ka transference! Fred is taken by this man. Never knew you swung that way, Freddy.'

Frederick grew tired of this. 'Oh, come, Eryn, you know as well as any of us that our people have had to outgrow antiquated labels. It's one of the first lessons we're taught. Gender, sexuality... We have been given a whole world of experiences to explore. It's about time the human world caught up with us.' He glanced up at Celeste, and pressed his hand on hers, which still rested on his shoulder. 'This is no different.'

Celeste nodded, but there was no concern in her eyes. She didn't doubt Frederick's feelings for her. 'What time do you intend to leave the nightclub?' she asked simply.

'Two?' Frederick suggested with a shrug. 'Seems a reasonable time. Any earlier and Will might be too cautious.'

'Very well. Theodor will make the arrangements for the test, and Eryn, you will contact Rochelle. We need to make sure any evidence disappears swiftly, however the outcome. And you, Frederick...' She helped him to his feet. 'I expect you to have a good time. But keep a close eye on him. The Book is vague on the specifics, and we cannot afford to waste this opportunity.'

'I know.'

'Then it is decided.' Celeste turned from him and over her shoulder Frederick caught sight of Eryn's look.

Frederick didn't bother hiding his smile. The old grudge still held sway in Eryn's heart. Even now, over two hundred years on, Eryn was convinced that at any moment Frederick would claim his rightful place alongside Celeste, giving her what she really wanted, her two life-companions by her side once more.

Frederick was quite happy for Eryn to hold the grudge, it made her careless and an easy target, but in truth Frederick had no interest in joining the Three.

His own mission far exceeded any pull the Three had. Like him they were a tool of fate, but unlike him they failed to realise that once the Seeker was found the Three, as a body, would be amazingly irrelevant.

11. The Fires of Hunger

The balcony at the rear of Zinc, like the other nightclubs along Lucy Road, overlooked Marine Parade and the Adventure Island amusement park. At the height of summer, the pavements would be crowded to overflowing, families coming and going, spending hard earned money in the arcades directly beneath the nightclubs, while others enjoyed the rides in the fairground. Pubs serviced those who preferred to sit in the sun and get pissed on expensive alcohol. But as night fell and Adventure Island closed, the seafront changed. Late night revellers hit the arcades, tanked up on alcohol and drugs, while boy racers in their pimped-up rides drove along the seafront showing off to all and sundry. From all over Essex young people congregated, from Hadleigh to Shoeburyness they came, barely legal teenagers and twenty-somethings looking to party. Once the arcades closed it was up to the nightclubs.

Frederick liked teenagers and twenty-somethings, they were so full of life, living it large without a care in the world. Sometimes they reminded him of his own people, albeit limited in their knowledge and experience of life. The balcony was full of mostly teens, some smoking, others merely enjoying the fresh air after the sweaty intensity of the club. Energy they might have had, but not much by way of deep conversation.

Frederick sat on the bench that ran the length of the balcony wall, listening to some guy moaning about his boyfriend who was, apparently, very unappreciative of him. Frederick wondered if it had anything to do with the guy's inability to shut up and let the other person speak. Will was inside the club, dancing with strangers, a plastic bottle of Smirnoff Ice in one hand. Watching Will from his vantage point on the bench, Frederick saw little of the man Stephen had told him about. The reserved man who was bogged down in family crises and work had given way to a party animal. Frederick wasn't complaining. It was a side he liked very much.

He glanced at the still rambling man, and shook his head. Little people with their small problems bored him. He stood up and re-entered the nightclub.

Some people danced on the small stage before the DJ's mixing deck, while the rest filled up the dance floor. Among the throng of people was Will, getting groinal with a woman and a young man who was barely eighteen. They were laughing and singing along to the latest chart topper, and Will tried to join in. He had the rhythm but he clearly didn't know the words of the song, but the two with him didn't seem to care. The young man was too busy trying to make a pass at Will to notice, and his female companion was caught up in egging him on.

Frederick stopped and watched for a moment, idly playing with the idea of the four of them returning to his place. He could teach them all a thing or two about pleasure thresholds... But no, he had no time for such frivolity tonight. This night belonged to him and Will, at least for a short while longer.

Will hadn't expected to go clubbing, so he wore his best suit out. The blazer had been left at Frederick's along with the rest of his gear, but he wore his waistcoat over his white shirt which was now open, revealing his sweaty chest. The teen leaned forward and shouted something into Will's ear, and for his troubles all he got was a shake of a head and a wink as Will sipped the vodka mix. The teen was clearly disappointed, but he laughed anyway and ran a hand down Will's chest.

Frederick was surprised by the twinge of jealousy he felt at seeing this, which was replaced by a sense of happiness when Will spotted him and waved him over.

Once on the dance floor Frederick wrapped an arm around Will's gyrating body.

'Hey, lover,' he said. 'Having a good time?'

'I really am,' Will said, planting his lips on Frederick's. 'Beats a night at the theatre.'

Frederick smiled and looked at the young man who had been trying his luck; he and his female friend had moved on to try and encourage someone else into his bed. 'Let's get out of here. Somewhere a little more private?'

Will's eyes were glazed over from too much drink. Frederick tensed in surprise as Will drove his hand inside Frederick's jeans. Will nodded, a look of relish on his face. Frederick pulled Will's hand out, and with a laugh, he led Frederick towards the stairs.

*

They were still warm from the heat of many dancing bodies and so barely felt the cold, the only evidence of the breeze was on their shirts; Frederick's billowed out as the cold air found its way in through the gaps between the buttons, and Will's still open shirt flapped behind him.

Frederick looked Will up and down, drawn to his nipples, now hardened by the cold. Will noticed and winked. He didn't seem as drunk as he did inside, which was just as well.

'You think I look good all sweaty?'

Frederick admired his chest, and ran a hand over it. 'I am not saying no.'

Will threw his head back and laughed, before leaning in and whispering in the way only drunk people could whisper. 'Wait until you see my scar.'

Frederick grinned. 'Hidden away, is it?'

Will took Frederick's hand and guided it down his groin. 'Could say that.'

'What's the time?'

Will shrugged, removed his phone from his trousers' pocket and consulted the digital readout on the screen. 'Almost two,' he said, flipping the phone open. He pressed a few buttons then closed the phone disappointedly. 'Thought Jake might have texted back, but *nada*.'

Frederick had been a little concerned when Will had insisted on sending Jake a text while they were on their way to the club, but Will promised to not mention any names. He would tell Jake all about it on Sunday when he returned home. For now, though, Jake would be quite happy to know that Will was having a good time.

'Seems you were right then. He's just leaving you to it.'

'Yeah, Jake's great like that, best friend a man could have. Was hoping he'd let me know how Curtis is, though.' The cold had clearly started getting to him, as Will began doing up his shirt. 'Still, things must be okay back home, otherwise he would have texted me, right?'

'That would follow, yes.'

'Good.' Will smiled broadly. 'Love that man to bits.'

Frederick pulled Will closer to him, and held him by his belt. He ran a hand across Will's naked torso. 'Competition?'

Will laughed. 'God no. More like a faithful dog.'

'Good.' Frederick kissed Will. They withdrew their tongues and looked each other in the eye.

'You still haven't explained all that oddness at the Residence. What kind of business are you in? That guy... Nate... gave me the impression that something very strange was going on. Something to do with me.'

Frederick placed a finger on Will's lips to silence him, silently cursing Nate. Unlike him to be so careless.

'Let's not spoil the night; we can discuss this in the morning... In my bed. I promise.' He nodded to his left. 'There's an alley over there. We can practice before we head back to mine if you'd like?'

'Don't need to tell me twice,' Will said and allowed himself to be led by Frederick.

It was as he had predicted, all Will needed was a bit of alcohol to loosen him up and he was ready to explode. The lure of sex. Best weapon a man had, human or not.

The alley was lit by only one lamp, the second having been smashed by vandals some time ago, and so Will and Frederick sank into the shadows, safe from the prying eyes of any potential voyeurs.

Frederick allowed himself to be pressed against the wall, feeling the hardness of the bricks against his back, matching the hardness coming from Will as he sandwiched Frederick with the wall. Will pushed his tongue into Frederick's mouth, grabbing his hand and placing it against the hardness in his trousers. Frederick closed his eyes, feeling his own pulse racing, massaging the material with his hand, Will's fingers entangled in his.

Frederick knew he was a liar. He hadn't meant to be, but his words to the Three had been full of falsehood. His seduction of Will went beyond the mission, preparing him for the test ahead. He wanted Will, and it wasn't until he felt Will's dick throbbing against his palm that he realised he always had, ever since he'd first bumped into Will almost a decade ago.

Whether the test proved him to be the Seeker or not, Frederick intended to keep Will. There was, to his mind, no room for discussion.

*

Desk duty bored Stewart Lumley; he was a beat officer, that's why he joined the police service in the first place; to be out there on the streets, keeping people safe and generally helping the public. But once again he'd pulled the short straw and was on desk duty. It could have been worse, he supposed, he could have been on the front desk talking to members of the public who came in to bitch about neighbours and the like. Okay, he considered with a sly smile, so maybe that would have been a little better. Anything would have been better than sitting at the desk with the footage of numerous surveillance cameras rooted through the large screen before him.

Watching CCTV was akin to watching paint dry, boring in the extreme. Nothing seemed to actually happen, despite the fact that the footage displayed had been signposted for special attention by various stations throughout Essex. Even when something did happen, all he had to do was inform his superiors and put a call through to dispatch who would then send officers out.

As he said, boredom city. Still, he had no choice. DI Swanson had assigned him the duty, and he knew he had to pay particular attention to the Lucy Road alley behind Saint John's Church, which had been routed through by his associate at the Control Centre in Southend. Right now, all he saw were two guys copping off. If he were that way inclined he'd at least be aroused by the sight, but as it was men did nothing for him, and seeing two blokes snogging merely made him feel indifferent.

He sat forward suddenly, as two burley and angry looking men stepped into view of the camera. This was what Swanson had warned him about.

He reached for his mobile; the call he had to make was private and he wasn't allowed to use HQ phones.

Even after three years he didn't fully understand the world he'd been initiated into, but he knew enough to know that the Three were taking a strong interest. He just hoped that by following Swanson's orders to the letter, he'd finally get an audience with the Three, which would hopefully lead to some real answers at last.

*

'Will!'

Jake awoke with a start, his hand reaching for Amy. It took him a moment to realise why she wasn't there. She was sleeping in her own bed, and he was sleeping in Will's.

He sat up, his breathing still coming in deep and jagged.

A dream.

He vaguely remembered, just on the edges of his consciousness. It had involved Will, he felt sure. He frowned, trying to remember. Will and he had been...

In bed together?

Jake looked to the left side of the bed, where only the crumpled duvet lay. He shook his head. No, that was mad, why would he dream of sharing the bed with Will? They hadn't done that since they were kids. Only...

The more he thought, the more he was sure they had been doing more than sharing a bed. They had been...

Jake pulled the duvet back, looked down at his softening dick.

'Betrayer,' he told it.

But it had just been a dream, it didn't mean anything. Just the unconscious mind, probably a strange interpretation of his concern for Will.

Jake reached over for his phone. It was just gone two. Which meant, presumably, Will was out on the town with Charlie.

Jake flopped back onto the bed, doubting he'd get much sleep again. Despite everything he'd told Amy, despite her almost convincing him, Jake knew his concerns weren't foolish.

Will being away with an unknown man was not a good thing.

These thoughts continued to run through his mind as his hand, almost as if it had a mind of its own, reached down to massage his dick.

*

Will's breathing became shallow and faster, and the throbbing increased beneath Frederick's palm. Their fingers tightened around each other, as Will guided Frederick's hand in the rhythm he liked.

Frederick had tried to unzip the trousers, but Will seemed quite happy to shoot his load in his boxers. He had his head back, neck arched, eyes closed, and therefore didn't see the two men step around the corner and into the alley. But Frederick saw them. Was expecting them.

He stopped the movement of his hand, and Will looked at him, his face close to ecstasy.

'Why... have you... stopped?' he asked between deep breaths.

Frederick didn't need to answer, instead the crunching of glass underfoot provided Will with all the response he needed.

He looked to the right as two others entered the opposite end of the alley. Like their two buddies, these two were just as big, their faces full of menace.

'You queer fuckers,' one of them said, his voice like gravel.

'Oh shit,' Will said softly, looking at Frederick, who pulled his hand away from Will's groin and stepped away from the wall.

The fear coming from Will was palpable, but this was just what Will needed. Frederick had to keep telling himself that.

The men drew closer, boxing them in. Frederick glanced at Will, who was now standing against the wall, showing no sign of being able to handle himself. It seemed Will needed a bit of nudging.

Before the two who entered the end of the alley could move any closer, Frederick was on them. He shot across the alley, shedding his fingernails like the skin of a snake, and talons made of bone, as sharp as razors, grew from the tips. He slashed the throat of one of the men, while simultaneously slamming his foot into the stomach of the other. The first reached for his throat, but he was far too late. Blood spewed out between his fingers and he dropped to his knees gagging for breath, and for his efforts he got nothing but blood bubbling out of his mouth.

Winded, the second staggered back, but before he could renew his own attack, Frederick plunged his fingers into the man's chest, smashing his chest bone along the way.

'What the fuck?' he heard from behind.

A pair of strong arms wrapped themselves around Frederick's torso, but Frederick's speed was beyond that of his assailant. He spun around so fast that the third man lost his grip and went careering into the wall. A crack echoed in the alley; the sound of the thug's head smashing against the jagged bricks.

Frederick looked down at the three who had fallen; two were dead, and the third was out cold, although Frederick didn't rate his chances of survival judging by the brain matter still clinging to the bricks.

The sound of scuffling alerted him to Will's own fight.

Will was on the ground, curling into a ball to protect himself from the boots that were slamming into his abdomen. The thug was laughing.

'You're nothing!' he said between laughs. 'We always knew you would be.'

Frederick didn't stop to process the meaning behind the words; he merely rushed across the alley, his concern for Will overriding his reasoning. He slammed his shoulder into the thug, sending the man against the far wall. But no sound of cracking bone came this time. Instead the thug had his arms out to cushion himself as he hit the wall. He turned and looked at Frederick. And smiled.

'Wrong again,' he said and launched himself.

Frederick was in the air and the two of them collided five feet above Will; the impact of their bodies sent them spinning and tumbling onto the cold concrete path. They scrambled to their feet, Frederick taken aback by the unexpected turn in the test. This was *not* what he and the Three had planned.

As they circled each other, Frederick noticed a tattoo just below the man's left ear. It showed the head of a lioness, a cobra wrapped around it.

The thug was a Sekhite.

Holding back was no longer an option. Feigning left, Frederick struck from the right, tearing his talons down the back of the Sekhite who had fallen for the misdirection. He arched in shock and pain, but before he could recover Frederick was on him, driving his fingers deep down the man's throat and ripping out his oesophagus through his mouth. The Sekhite fell, his life ebbing away by the second.

Frederick dropped to his knees beside the Sekhite, and brought his mouth over the dying man's. His tongue lapped up the blood frothing inside the shredded mouth cavity, and he closed his eyes.

If the followers of the Brotherhood knew of the test then it could only mean someone had betrayed the Three, and the Sekhite's lifeblood would reveal who. If Frederick was fast enough.

A hand touched his shoulder, and a quavering voice asked, 'Frederick?', but Frederick was so caught up in the hunger that everything else failed next to it.

Enraged, Frederick lashed out, delighted by the feel of his talons penetrating more flesh.

He forced himself to stop once he had the information he needed; or at least the face of the one who had betrayed them. He lifted his head, licking the blood still on his lips, his eyes closed.

Behind his eyelids, Frederick saw a face he knew well enough, the black hair with the stupid electric blue hi-lites, the arrogance splashed all across the young face. Frederick didn't understand why Eryn would do such a thing; she was one of the Three! It made no sense to...

Frederick's eyes opened, and he looked down at the destroyed man beneath him. Then over at the other three thugs who had been dispatched so easily. That made four. And there had only been four attackers. So who was the fifth person he had shredded with his talons in?

A dead weight hit his heart and Frederick turned around, his talons pulling back into the sheaths of his fingers.

Lying on the ground behind him, a pool of blood forming from the gaping wound in his neck, was Will. Still on his knees, Frederick scrambled to Will's side.

Will blinked, his eyes drifting everywhere, trying to focus on one thing. With much effort he looked at Frederick. He reached out a hand, his fingers gently touching the redness on Frederick's cheek.

'Tears of...' Will coughed. 'Blood?'

Frederick placed a hand on his face and felt the warm substance. He had drunk so much from the Sekhite that his contact lenses could not contain the excess blood now flowing behind his eyes. He shook his head sadly.

'This was not... You were supposed to be...'

'What...' Another cough, this time accompanied by bloody spittle. 'What are you? A vam...' More blood. Will forced the word out. 'Vampire?'

'No, yes... Well, technically yes, but... No, not exactly.' Frederick wasn't sure what to say. Will was dying; he had slashed a vital artery in Will's neck. Centuries of practice meant that Frederick knew how to strike the killing blow every time. But he couldn't lose Will; not now that he had only just found him.

'You're a... fucking vampire?' Even as he died, drowning in his own blood, he laughed. 'Why...? Why couldn't you leave me... alone?'

'I'll explain all later, I promise,' Frederick said, lowering his face towards Will's.

'Later?' Will coughed up more blood. 'Everything's going cold... Is it cold?' He reached a feeble hand to stop the descent of Frederick's face, but Frederick just brushed it away.

'I'm so sorry, Will, I was wrong. I'll make it up to you. But first I must do this.'

Will tried to pull away, but Frederick held his head still and forced Will's mouth open with his tongue. Through the viscous blood rising from his throat, Frederick's own tongue found its way beneath Will's and, like a snake striking out, he pierced the lingual artery. A minute orifice opened at the tip of Frederick's tongue.

Leech-like, the blood was sucked directly from Will's tongue and into that of Frederick's.

But as Will's heart slowed close to stopping, Frederick ceased sucking, and pulled his tongue from Will's mouth.

He looked down at the pale face, Will's almost lifeless eyes looking up at the stars above. Frederick wasted no time. He placed his tongue deep within the gash on Will's neck, and a geyser of blood spewed from Frederick directly into Will.

The eternal kiss was given, and Will succumbed to the First Death.

12. All for the Mission

The clean-up crew arrived within ten minutes, to find Frederick kneeling beside Will's corpse. The nightclubs were still open, and those rare few who came out onto Lucy Road were either laughing too much or engaged in drink-induced arguments to notice the commotion in the alley along the way, not that there was much of a commotion, of course, since the clean-up crew were very good at what they did.

Their black van pulled up on the road behind the church, adjacent to the alley, and the back doors opened, spewing out three men. Frederick looked up, and smiled slightly at their black outfits. Minimum visibility was the order of the day in their job. They quickly got to picking up the corpses, dumping them in the back of the van. They came to get Will, but Frederick held them back with a hand.

'Sir?' Just by his stature Frederick had spotted Callum Flynn immediately. He was a specialist, and only ever called on directly by Celeste.

'Wait,' Frederick said. He reached into Will's trousers' pocket. He pulled out the mobile, not too surprised to see the screen cracked slightly. He deposited it in his own pocket. He then removed Will's wallet.

'This is most irregular,' Callum said, again looking at his three colleagues who were still clearing up the blood and viscera. 'We have specific orders from the Three. No trace to be left.' He nodded at his men to continue, and they strapped canisters to their backs.

'I know your orders,' Frederick pointed out. 'But this is a special case. And you know who I am.' He stood up, and looked down at the much shorter man. 'Do you really want to come up against me?'

Callum held his hands up. 'No need to be hostile, sir, I'm just saying. This is damned irregular.'

'Then that's how it will be.'

He grabbed his leather jacket off the ground and left the clean-up crew to it. He stopped on the way out of the alley and glanced up at the CCTV camera. He wondered how much of this Swanson got. Hopefully she had already arranged for the tape to be removed and replaced with pre-recorded footage of the alley, if not then she might have seen him remove the things from Will's pocket.

It didn't matter really. She knew better than to say anything.

*

He crouched on the sand and pebbles, looking out across the Thames Estuary. He had got as far as Westcliff before he realised he needed to wash the blood from his lips. It was almost three in the morning and the seafront was pretty much empty, but for the occasional person leaving the Maxims Casino. He had received a few odd looks, but his mind had been elsewhere and it didn't occur to him that he was walking around with blood drying over his mouth.

He splashed water over his face and washed away the evidence of his zealous feeding.

He had been sure that Will was to be the Seeker. That he carried *the* ka inside his own human soul was beyond doubt, and according to the Book of Sekhmet only one such ka was to be reincarnated.

Not for the first time he wished Melinda the Scribe was still among them; her linguistic skills were second to none. As the Ancient had told him he would, Frederick had found her once the Sumerian language was rediscovered. For over a hundred years they had worked side by side, in secret, uncovering the mysteries contained within the Book. Together they had learned of the truth of their origins. When they had taken this to the Three, it was quickly decided by Celeste that Melinda had to be removed permanently. Celeste trusted only Frederick, for his heart was of Celeste, but Melinda was a scholar and her knowledge could be bought or tortured out of her by the right people.

Frederick could forgive Celeste many things, but killing Melinda was not one of them. Although she had taught him how to read and translate the Neo-Sumerian and the dozen other languages the Book was written in, he didn't have Melinda's skill.

And now, as he looked out over the water, he had to wonder. Had he misinterpreted the writings in the Book?

The test was simple. Put the suspected Seeker into a situation where the fires of hunger would take over. His people didn't need blood, not anymore, but every now and then it was nice to feast upon it, for ultimately they were the offspring of a blood drinker; Onuris the First Vampire. But over the centuries they became civilised, resisted the hunger that once drove their ancestors. Alas, still the hunger came on them when they were threatened, when their very lives were at risk. It was hoped to be the same for the Seeker, that with his life threatened the hunger would manifest.

This had not happened. Instead Will had acted like a human. Out of his depth and transfixed by the horror he witnessed, until he ended up one among many victims of the hunger that could take hold of upiór.

Frederick looked up at the stars. Celeste would not be happy about what he had done. The Rebirth of an upiór was not to be taken lightly. There were strict rules governing such an event, rules that had been in place for over two hundred years, but Frederick had thrown those rules aside, driven by his desire to keep Will.

In three nights Will would be one of them; he may not have been the Seeker, but he surely would stand by Frederick's side from thereon.

*

'Where the hell have you been?' Jake snapped as Lawrencia walked through the front door. 'You told Will—'

'Well, I'm here now. What's the problem?'

Jake just glared at her. 'Whatever. I'm going out, you stay here with your son. And you better not let Jimmy anywhere near here. Right?'

Lawrencia looked like she was about to argue, but instead she just nodded. 'Where is he?'

Jake nodded at the lounge, while he grabbed his jacket and put it on. 'In there, watching CBeebies.' He opened the door. 'See you in a bit, champ,' he called.

'Bye, Undle Jake!'

Jake smiled, then glared at Lawrencia again before she could smile with him. 'I won't be long, so make sure you're here when I get back.'

He didn't wait for an answer, he simply slammed the door shut behind him and stalked away from the house.

He'd barely had any sleep, and what he did have he didn't want to remember. He knew what had happened last night, what he had done, and who was on his mind as he'd done it, but this morning he had decided he wouldn't – couldn't! – think like that again. He was with Amy, he loved being with Amy, and Will was... his best mate. And that was all!

Jake pulled out his phone and dialled a number.

'All right, Jakey-boy!' Mikey said. 'What's shaking?'

'What you up to?'

'Not a lot. Misses is out, so I'm—'

'Free? Cool. Drink at The Chancery?'

'What? Bit early, isn't it?'

Jake shrugged. 'Must be after midday somewhere.'

Mikey was silent a moment, then, 'All right then, why not? Reckon I can convince them to give us a cheeky pint or two.'

That sounded just the right ticket to Jake.

He'd soon forget about last night.

*

Frederick had not been able to sleep, and as he entered the private meeting room of the Three the following morning, he was fresh and alert. Still he could feel the fresh blood coursing through his body. Celeste had tried to contact him last night, initially by phone, but once she realised he was not taking any calls she called him through the blood bond they shared. Her voice had echoed in his mind, but he was too stoked by his gorging to make any sense. Celeste knew but chose to not mention it; no doubt Callum had already informed the Three how two of the dead had been drained.

There were no rules on the consumption of blood, but there were warnings. They had all seen the result of too much blood, how some of their people had become addicted to the life fluid. In their world it was called *haemomania*, a strong psychological craving for blood. These blood junkies rarely ended well, and were a cautionary tale for those who liked to consume blood just that bit too much. Frederick knew he wasn't anywhere close to that depth, but for hours he was intoxicated by the amount of blood in his veins, and needed to come back down before he went to meet with the Three.

Now he was at a manageable level once more, although the new blood made him more alert than usual. Which was no bad thing. He had decided to keep an eye on Eryn, to let her play her hand before Frederick made a move against her. Eryn had been one of the Three since the beginning, and for her to betray them made no sense. And worse, why would she enlist the services of a Sekhite?

Frederick opened the door, ignoring the welcomes of Nate, and walked straight through the chamber and into the private room. He saw Eryn sitting there, talking quietly to Theodor. Celeste had yet to arrive. Eryn looked up and smiled.

'Would you care for a glass of blood wine?' she asked, standing and walking over to the cabinet that contained decanters of various blood types.

Frederick swallowed. The thought of more blood made him nauseous. He had had his fill.

'I think I'll pass this time.'

'I don't doubt it, Freddy,' Eryn said, making a display of pouring some blood wine into two glasses. One for her and one for Theodor. 'So, what went wrong then?'

Frederick bit back his response. Eryn knew exactly what had gone wrong. Frederick knew how the Sekhites would benefit from the death of the real Seeker, but he couldn't see how Eryn would benefit. Maybe she merely wanted to spite Frederick?

For hundreds of years Eryn had played second place to Frederick, and an occasional feud had grown out of that resentment. It was only Eryn who had noticed Frederick's attraction to Will, although she had stupidly thought it a case of ka transference. Frederick knew it would not be beneath Eryn to have Will removed simply to get at Frederick; but to use a Sekhite to do so was a bold move indeed.

If Will was proved to be the Seeker, then everything the Sekhites believed would crash down. It made no sense, though. As one of the Three, Eryn knew the truth, that the Sekhite way was built on lies perpetuated by the leader of the Brotherhood of Sekhmet. Eryn had been the most vocal when Frederick had first told the Three of Will, and even after meeting Will, Eryn was not convinced about him.

No, the only thing that made sense was that Eryn had decided that a Sekhite was the best tool in eliminating Will as a personal attack on Frederick. Only... somehow Frederick was sure he was missing something important.

'I'll discuss it when Celeste arrives,' Frederick said, finally. 'Since it involves news of the Seeker.'

Eryn froze mid-step, and looked sharply at Frederick. Frederick held her gaze, and allowed the younger upiór to carry on with handing a drink to Theodor. He looked from his twin to Frederick and back again. The warning was unmistakable. It was impossible to believe Theodor would also conspire against the prophecy; his loyalty to the Three and to Celeste was second only to Frederick's. It was more likely he was simply warning Eryn to not push.

'And here I am,' Celeste said, gliding into the room. She swept past Frederick, placing a hand on his shoulder briefly, and helped herself to a glass of actual wine.

Once she was seated, Frederick explained all that had happened the previous night, omitting only how Will had died. He gambled that the CCTV had been wiped, and so told them that the Sekhite had killed Will before Frederick could stop him. Once he had finished, silence fell on the room; even Eryn had little to say, although it was clear she was itching to say something, to put forward her own theory before anyone else. But she had enough sense to remain quiet, for to speak before Celeste would arouse immediate suspicion.

'Why was Willem also drained?' Celeste asked, finally.

Frederick swallowed, feeling shame for his lies. 'The hunger got the better of me, I fear. Draining the Sekhite was not enough...' He hung his head, and mumbled, 'A moment of weakness I regret.'

For a moment longer there was silence, and Frederick looked up. Eryn eyed him suspiciously, but said nothing, keeping her thoughts secret for a change. Theodor raised an eyebrow at Frederick and shook his head, disappointed that one so close to the Three would give in to the hunger so easily, then turned to Celeste.

'This is grave news indeed, Frederick,' she said shortly. 'That the Brotherhood should know of the test...'

'And, possibly worse, that they know you're in town,' Frederick added, looking directly at Eryn.

She narrowed her eyes in response, but otherwise gave no indication she understood the implication Frederick was throwing her way. Frederick looked back at Celeste.

'They will surely take advantage of this. The Three are very rarely in the same place for any given length of time. The Brotherhood has been growing in strength these last few decades...'

'And soon they will strike,' Eryn offered up. Frederick wasn't too sure, but he thought he heard a threat in her tone. Neither Celeste nor Theodor appeared to register the threat however, so Frederick marked it down to his perceptions being clouded by his knowledge of Eryn's part in the ruination of the test. Whatever her part was exactly, was something Frederick would have to find out.

'Let them. They have foolishly shown their hand now,' Celeste said. 'And so we will be ready. We cannot leave Canvey for at least a week, since we have many audiences prearranged and cannot disappoint the upiór in this county. And I have a personal meeting with Lady Isobel which cannot be simply cancelled. If we leave suddenly then the Sekhites will know we are aware of them as they are of us.' She stood up and looked to each of her inner circle one by one. 'We will not be cowed by the threat posed by the Brotherhood, not now that we are so close to the time of Onuris' return. Neither will we be caught unawares; preparations will be made. The Brotherhood will not find us such an easy target this time. We removed them once, we can do so again.'

She walked over to Frederick and laid a hand on him. 'Keep looking for the Seeker; the Ancient said you will find him and you shall. Just try to make it within the next week if you can,' she added, bestowing upon Frederick her most beautiful smile.

*

Frederick remembered the moment very clearly; it was a day that was destined to change his life.

He had been summoned to Romania by Wamukota the Ancient, the oldest of their kind. Why Wamukota wished to see him, Frederick did not know, but it was a calling he could not ignore. Wamukota was hiding out in a small village in Moldavia, which in 1790 was a precarious place to be, situated as it was in the middle of the war between Russia, Austria and Turkey. The newly-christened upiór (a Slavic term coined by the Three to distance their people from the savage vampire of myth) had only just come out of its own war, which saw the birth of the Three, and no upiór wished to enter a war between humans, so Wamukota had chosen his hiding place well.

Nonetheless, the Ancient wished to see Frederick and so he had no choice but to endure the perilous journey across Russia. He had felt young when he left Celeste's side in France, but by the time he reached Tuzara, Frederick felt very old and knew his first preternatural body was dying. Before starting on the final leg of his journey he had visited the small town of Jassy, and there espied a fresh nineteen-year-old male who would make the perfect recipient for his first transference. An act that would see the end of his life as Frederick Holtzrichter.

Having undergone transference many times since then, Frederick found it funny how scared he had been by the thought at first. Being so close to another male was not a notion he liked to entertain, but Celeste had coached him well, and he understood that as upiór he had to put away the morality and ethics of his human life. First, though, he had to meet with Wamukota.

*

'The Book of Origin? Of course I know of it,' Frederick said.

There was not a single upiór alive who did not know of the Book; ever since his Rebirth, Frederick had heard of the mythical book, lost some two hundred years ago. It was purported to be the history of their people, as written by the Ancient, but many rumours and stories circulated about both the Book and the Ancient, and most of them were contradictory.

For two years Frederick had tried to find everything he could about the Book, ever since he'd seen a few translated pages in England. Despite the tenacity of his search, there was only one thing about which he was certain; upiór bore a connection to the little-known Egyptian God Sekhmet.

'The Book was, ah, returned to me almost a year ago,' Wamukota said.

Frederick stared at him in shock. The Ancient was small and frail, his brown skin like brittle paper, but his brown eyes were alight with life and intelligence. Frederick leaned forward in his chair, his hand tightening around the flagon which still contained wine untouched by his lips. He could barely believe it.

'It was in the possession of a man called Edward Lomax,' Wamukota continued, his long white hair being blown into his face by the breeze. 'He attempted to use his knowledge of the Book to blackmail me into removing someone called Theodor. I believe he is known to you?'

Frederick knew Theodor well, another consort of Celeste's, and now a member of the Three. He knew little about Theodor, though, but had heard talk of Lomax before, and was not surprised to hear the English upiór was still pursuing his private vendetta against Theodor. Although Frederick was still none the wiser as to the source of the vendetta.

The Ancient smiled. 'This Lomax soon found that, although I may be old, I am by no means weak. Ever since my book was stolen in 1588 I have been continuing to write notes, detailing my dreams and visions of our shared history. Of times before Ancient Egypt.'

'Before?' Frederick balked.

'Yes, but let that not concern you now. For the past year I have been translating my notes into Sumerian and various other languages I have learned in my long life, putting them into the book, trying to make some kind of order from them. It has been hard work, and remains incomplete. But now my time has come. This body is wearing thin and, after almost four thousand years of life, it is time to die. Finally.'

The enormity of the moment overwhelmed Frederick and he could find no words to say, yet Wamukota just smiled at him. The smile put Frederick's mind at peace. He could not begin to understand what it had to be like, to live for so long, but he suspected he too would welcome the end when it came.

'Why...' He swallowed and tried again. 'Why have you called me here? What can I do?'

'I wish to pass my work on to you. You will finish what I have started, compile my notes, make sense of the chaos.'

Frederick's throat was dry. He put the flagon to his lips and sipped the wine, which was somewhat thicker in texture than he was used to.

Spoiled by the wine produced in France, no doubt, but he didn't much care for Moldavian wine. The Ancient watched him with a smile.

'Why me?'

'Because learning the truth has become an obsession for you.' The Ancient raised his eyebrows. 'You think I am unaware of your intensive search? You have found much translated material, badly translated material. But now you shall have the original book, notes and all.'

'But I know nothing of this... what did you call it? Sumerian? I have never even heard of the language.'

'No, it is the language of my ancestors. Dead now, much like your own Old Prussian, but in time it will be discovered again, and when it is you will find the best translator to help you. It is not all in Sumerian, though, some of it is Egyptian, and my own blood will give you a start in understanding the hieroglyphs of my people. As for the other languages... well,' and here the cracked face smiled, 'they will give you reason to expand your mind.'

Frederick thought his mind had expanded more than enough since becoming an upiór, but one word struck him. 'Your blood?'

'Yes.' The Ancient indicated the flagon in Frederick's hand, and Frederick looked down at it. The reason for its strange thickness suddenly became apparent. 'That is not merely wine, but my own blood.' Wamukota leaned forward, his old bones creaking. 'In time, in 221 years to be exact, you will also need my blood to help you find the Seeker.'

'The Seeker? You mean Seker?'

Wamukota shook his head and laughed. 'Seker! That is very good. Once upon a time I...' He stopped laughing abruptly. 'Times now gone. No, not Seker. The Seeker.' The Ancient nodded. 'The Book will explain this to you. One day the Seeker shall appear, and with my blood in your veins you will know him.'

*

Frederick had done everything he had promised, studied the Book, completed the notes as best he could, given that most of them burned with the Ancient in the Moldavian monastery, enlisted the help of Melinda too. For over two hundred years Frederick had believed in the mission Wamukota had given him, and he had never once told anyone, not even Celeste, that the blood of the Ancient filled his veins. He had been so sure, nine years ago, that he had felt the Seeker in Will. But then last night happened.

He had confused his own feelings with his mission, and it had cost the life of an innocent man. Frederick could not let Will's life end so abruptly.

So now he waited. It was almost twenty-four hours since Will had been killed, and he stood at the edge of the Lucy Road alley.

Soon the first stage of Rebirth would begin, and Will would enter the pontus, the netherworld between humanity and becoming a true upiór.

13. Hunted

Frederick sat on the narrow wall and glanced around; the differing sounds of various songs mingled in the air coming from the nightclubs and, once again, much like the night before, the alley was deserted. The clubs didn't close until four and so Frederick was left alone to do as he wanted. He had already smashed the second lamp, casting the alley in a pit of shadow. As an upiór, he didn't need light by which to see clearly.

Already he had placed several plastic packs in strategic spots along the alley, and he had but one more to do. This he tied to the lamppost. Once done he jumped off the wall and landed softly on the ground.

Each of the small packs contained blood, taken from one of the secret blood banks that were used to source the food of upiór who lived in Essex. Such blood banks were located all across the world; just one of the initiatives the Three had set up to prevent the hunger overcoming their people. It was true that upiór had mostly outgrown their *need* for blood, but there was barely an upiór alive who didn't like the rich taste of blood – after all, despite everything, they were still descended from vampires and, as Stoker had written, 'blood is life'. And so fresh blood was always on hand for those who wanted it. For a small price, of course.

Much like the human world, supply and demand was the stock and trade of many businesses run by upiór. But the Three curtailed any potential unscrupulous business taking place, so that if money was not available then upiór could trade their services for a pack of blood. It had taken some wrangling, but he had managed to convince Rhys Rubery, the owner of the Chalkwell blood bank, to allow him ten packs. Rhys was one of the thousands of Initiates seeded throughout the human world;

humans who aspired to the life of an upiór, a reward they would get once they had proven their loyalty. Unlike most Initiates, though, Rhys did not partake in Red Source, the name given to the preternatural blood by the Initiates who drank it. He was saving himself for rebirthing.

As far as Rhys knew, Frederick was on a secret mission for the Three; this was enough to ensure his cooperation and silence. He would never question a mission for the Three and knew better than to discuss it with any other, and so word that Frederick had procured so much blood would never reach the Three.

He looked around the alley. Blood packs led from the lamppost and along the alley to his borrowed van, which was waiting outside the church, the backdoor wide open. Inside which was a pile of five more packs, enough to entice the thirstiest upiór. Especially one not fully formed.

Soon the first stage of the Rebirth would take place, and Frederick had to ensure that Will's shayde did not stray far. For the first night he would be a thing of no substance, merely a shadow of a ka driven by a thirst for life. His mortal body, as well as those of the hired thugs and the Sekhite, had been incinerated as per the standard procedure of the clean-up. Such an ignoble end for any life, but it was better that than any trace of upiór be given to the human world.

Already there were some in that world who suspected, and the only way to contain the potential threat posed by such people was an exercise in damage limitation. Empirical evidence of otherworldly happenings was destroyed by the clean-up crew, leaving nothing but idle gossip and hearsay. Will and the thugs would soon be on the list of missing people in the UK.

It seemed very likely that people would miss Will and start poking about, but they'd find nothing but a trail that ended outside a nightclub in Southend. Already today a few texts had been sent to Will's phone which Frederick kept in the inside pocket of his leather jacket. Jake was persistent, and on at least one occasion he had tried to ring, too. But as with all those who fell afoul of upiór, the relatives and/or friends left behind would eventually give up the searching and mourn the loss.

Usually a Rebirth would happen under controlled circumstances, supervised by a member of the Rebirth Council. The carefully chosen soon-to-be fledgling upiór would be taken to a secret place where their Rebirth could be contained. But Will's was born from tragedy and desperation, and worse, was unfortunately out in the open. It could so easily attract the attentions of other upiór, which would most certainly lead to the involvement of the Three. Frederick could not risk that, and so he hoped that the packs of blood would be enough to trap the shayde in the van, which he would then take to a secret location.

Short of bringing a human to sacrifice to the shayde, there was little else Frederick could do. He just hoped it would be enough. And if not, then he could always bring Stephen directly into things earlier than planned.

Frederick looked up sharply, feeling an odd prickling at the edge of his consciousness. Turning on his heels, he narrowed his eyes to see what he could only feel.

Someone was watching him.

He closed his eyes, trying to zone in on the presence he felt. It was definitely human, but there was something else there, too. A human presence would barely register on the periphery of an upiór's senses, especially not one with Frederick's limited psychic ability, however this was a little more than human, but not quite an upiór. It could only mean one thing.

There was a hunter in town.

'Damn it,' Frederick hissed.

The hunter couldn't have picked a worse time to scent an upiór. And Frederick could not risk a confrontation now, not as Will's shayde was about to enter the pontus.

With speed that surpassed that of any normal human, Frederick hared down Lucy Road and broke right. He slowed down at the bottom of the sloping street and came out on Marine Parade. Even at this time of the morning people still wandered. Across the road several people sat on the small wall, joking and talking while friends went skinny dipping in the sea beyond.

A properly trained hunter would never attack in the open, instead they would follow an upiór into a back street or some other secluded spot. Most hunters had a stroke of arrogance about them, believing themselves better than any upiór by virtue of the human blood that ran through their veins. As such they were over confident and prone to fall into the simplest of traps.

Frederick suspected this hunter would be no different, and so he continued along the seafront, passing the closed arcades, nodding a passing hello to the random people who emerged from the smaller clubs that didn't quite qualify for the prestige of Lucy Road. All the while he could feel the hunter at his back.

*

He came to the gates of Southchurch Hall Gardens and stopped. Woodgrange Drive was mostly a residential street, covering the length from Southend through to Thorpe Bay, and as such it was not well suited for taking care of an ill-fated hunter. However, the parkland area beyond the closed gates was big enough to allow for quick disposal without disturbing the local residents.

For show, he lifted his head and pretended to sniff the air, snapping his head left. From the point of view of the hunter it would appear that the upiór prey had caught the scent of fresh blood, which made removing the upiór a necessity. Frederick smiled to himself and leaped over the closed gates, landing softly on the other side.

The parkland was in darkness, which suited Frederick's purpose. He walked up the path towards the grassy mound, pretending to stalk something. He stopped and sniffed, then shot right and dived into the small clump of trees. Once submerged behind the green foliage, he came to a standstill and turned. And waited.

The hunter came into the opening a short time later, half crouching, wooden stake raised in preparation. Frederick could not believe what he was seeing.

He watched the hunter a little longer, drawn by a sense of familiarity. At first Frederick had been expecting to see Maia, but this young man was certainly not the anticipated hunter.

Frederick shook his head. It didn't matter. The world could always do with one less hunter.

Purposely, he moved back into a less dense space and stepped on a fallen twig. He froze as the hunter spun to face him. Feigning surprise,

Frederick turned and fled further into the trees. The hunter pursued him.

The chase went on for ten minutes, with Frederick slowing his pace from time to time, allowing the hunter to get close, before heading off in a different direction. Frederick was very disappointed in the hunter's performance. He had fought several hunters over the years, and as the offspring of an upiór and a mortal they had inherited some preternatural abilities which tended to make them at least a little formidable, but this hunter seemed to have inherited nothing. He had no real speed, and very little awareness that he was being played with. A proper hunter would have been onto Frederick by now.

Bored already, he decided it was time to call it. He had much more important things to do that morning, paramount among them was returning to Lucy Road before Will's shayde supped on all the blood packs he'd left there. Even sleep would have been more involving.

Once more he allowed the hunter to close in, and contrived to fall over a stump. Finally, the hunter was on him, pinning Frederick down with his knees on Frederick's outstretched arms. He looked up at the young face in horror. And it really was a young face. The kid could have been no more than sixteen, the soft fluff running along his jaw line making him seem even younger.

'Die, blood sucker, die!' the boy hissed, slamming the wooden stake directly into Frederick's heart. The boy jumped to his feet, looking down at Frederick as he screamed out, no doubt expecting him to dissipate in a puff of smoke and dust or something. The boy grimaced, and muttered, 'From dust you came, to dust you will return.'

Frederick appreciated the poetry, but it was time the hunter was educated properly. He stopped his fake screaming abruptly, and looked down at the protruding piece of wood.

'Hmm,' he said, chewing his bottom lip. 'Not really working, eh?'

The hunter clearly had no idea what was going on. His smooth face was awash with confusion. Frederick slowly got to his feet, and touched the blood spreading on his white jumper.

'This is going to be a bastard to get out, you know,' he said conversationally. He yanked the stake out with a gasp, and winked at the boy. 'Wooden stakes not going to do the job, I'm afraid. Hurts, but that's about it. Sorry.'

'That's not my only weapon,' the hunter said in what he probably thought was a brazen tone. To Frederick it just sounded sad and weak.

The hunter launched himself at Frederick, leg raised, but Frederick was faster and used the leg to spin the hunter around into the nearest tree, smashing him against the trunk like a soft toy.

Ribs broken, the boy crumpled onto the earth, gasping for breath. With each gasp, the intense pain registered on his face.

Frederick knelt beside him. 'I'm sorry, but you chose this life, and for every action there is a consequence. For instance, a rebirth is soon to take place, and it occurs to me that you would make quite a good first feast.'

He grabbed hold of the boy and dragged him to his feet. 'Come on. You think you've made a mess of my shirt, wait until Will gets a hold of...' He stopped, and tilted his head to one side. 'There is something of Maia about you. Why is that?'

The boy spat out blood, and with it the word, 'Bitch'.

Frederick nodded. 'Ah, she trained you? Right, well, I think you've been had. Only...' Something was not right here. 'There's more to it than that, isn't there?' He looked closer at the pained face, and it came to him. He let the boy fall to the ground. 'You look a lot like her. Your sister?'

The boy nodded. 'And I know...' He gasped for air, trying to shift his weight off his broken ribs, but with every movement, waves of pain surged through his body. 'I know who you are!'

'Yes, well that would follow. She sent you after me, didn't she? That still doesn't explain why I could sense her in you. You have no preternatural blood in your veins.'

The boy shook his head, his eyes rolling in their sockets. He was on the verge of passing out, but his anger kept him conscious. 'Transfusion. Lomax taught her how...' He coughed and spat out more blood.

Frederick understood. Maia had given some of her blood to her brother, and sent him after Frederick. But to what end? She must have known the boy would be no match for Frederick. But the mention of Lomax... An upiór working with a hunter was almost unheard of. But if any upiór was going to do so, it would be Lomax.

Which was bad news for everybody. Including the Three. Especially Theodor.

'I'm not a great believer in reincarnation, well, except one special case, but if you happen to get a second chance at life, I'd strongly suggest you find Maia. She needs a good killing.'

Frederick lifted the stake, sickened by the horror in the boy's eyes. The ersatz hunter was in much pain, and had been little more than a dupe. Frederick knew he ought to spare his life, give the boy a chance to get even with Maia. But...

A brief thought passed him by. Turning the boy into an upiór would have been even more poetic than the comment about dust, sending the brother after the sister amused Frederick. She certainly had it coming. But no. One unauthorised Rebirth was enough, and he didn't want to push it. Besides, he had more important things to concern himself with, and allowing the boy to live would have been a distraction.

'Last lesson,' he said. 'Wooden stakes are useless on my people. Not something a hunter ought to use, still *suum cuique*.' Frederick smiled at the boy's confusion, so he said, 'To each his own.'

Without further preamble, he brought the stake down, splintering the wood through the boy's breast bone and directly into his heart.

*

The acrid smell of burned plastic assaulted his olfactory system the second he stepped into the alley. Melted and scrunched up, drained of every drop of blood, the packs lay discarded on the alley pavement. He shook his head, letting out a hiss of frustration and rushed over to the van. The back doors were still open, the pile of blood packs empty.

Frederick closed his eyes, hoping to be able to reach out to the shayde of the fledgling he'd made, but there was nothing. No sense of Will at all. He didn't really think there would be; the psychic connection between maker and fledgling did not come about until after the new upiór emerged from the pontus.

Frederick had thought he was being optimistic with ten packs, but he had underestimated Will's need. He had overseen many Rebirths and had never seen such a thirst before. Something told him the shayde was still out there.

Frederick turned to one of his peoples' more vulgar abilities, the one he'd pretended to use when luring the 'hunter' in. He sniffed, and immediately caught the whiff of fresh blood on the breeze. Nostrils open, he set off tracking the scent down.

*

He finally came to a house, in which only one light was on. Looking around, making sure no one else was watching, he quickly scaled the drainpipe. When they wanted to be, upiór could be extremely light and weigh almost nothing, but as with most of their preternatural abilities it took much concentration. He stepped on the exterior windowsill and crouched down to look through the net curtain.

At first he didn't see it. All he saw was a darkened bathroom, lit only by the light coming from the landing beyond. The bathroom was clean, with an overflowing washing basket in the corner nearest the door. It was near the basket that he first saw it; the shadow of a man stretched from the doorway, the 'head' enlarged along the width of the straw basket and the soiled clothes on top. There was no one standing in the doorway to project such a shadow, it just stretched out of its own accord. Most people would have been puzzled by it, but Frederick knew he'd found Will's shayde.

With a sense of revulsion he didn't know he could feel, Frederick realised what the shayde was doing. Atop the washing was a pair of knickers, stained by the residual menstrual blood left over by a badly applied sanitary pad, and the area of the shadow's mouth was…

Frederick pulled back. He'd seen enough.

There was no way Frederick could hold Will responsible for the actions of the shayde. It was a base creature led only by its most carnal need, no more aware than a plant soaking up the rays of the sun.

Frederick couldn't remember what had happened during his time in the pontus back in Prussia, but he hoped he hadn't done anything so disgusting. He was glad he didn't remember; some things were best left unknown. He just hoped it would be the same for Will.

14. Without a Will

Jake wasn't sure what woke him up first. The blazing light forcing its way through his eyelids, the sound of plastic crashing against metal, or the shrill voice breaking in from a distant, but clearly not distant enough, place.

For a moment, while his mind shifted from unconscious to conscious, he remained as he was. Lying on the couch, eyes closed, trying to reclaim the echo of a dream that was even now slipping through the gaps.

All he could recall was that it involved Will and it wasn't good; not exactly a nightmare, but an anxious dream. Which was better than the dream he'd had the night before. Nonetheless, the anxiety remained as his cognitive brain attempted to engage with the real world.

He still hadn't heard from Will since that text on Friday night. A day had passed since then, and nothing more was heard. Jake hoped it was simply due to Will enjoying himself so much with Charlie, as Amy insisted, but a large part of him still doubted it. Will had not answered a single text Jake had sent yesterday, and on the few occasions he tried to ring Will's mobile, first there had simply been no answer, and he was shifted to the answer machine, and then the phone line had been dead.

That weighed heavily on Jake's mind; Will was not the kind of guy to ignore calls, and it seemed unlikely he would forget to charge the phone. Thus, the anxiety which had translated into a dream about... Jake had no idea, just a sense that it was bad.

He opened his eyes slowly, now that they had adjusted a little to the light, but not quite as adjusted as he would have liked since he had to turn his head away from direct exposure. Lawrencia had no doubt decided it was a good idea to open the curtains of the lounge, heedless of how it might affect the man sleeping on the sofa. Of course, the day that Lawrencia had a thought that did not centre on her would be a red-letter day, and Jake would make sure he made a note of it. As it was, he had been rudely awoken by the light and Lawrencia's carelessness and was not particularly happy about it.

In the middle of the lounge was Curtis, still wearing his pyjama top, his Pampas Pull-Ups hanging between his legs like some overfilled colostomy bag. Naturally the thought of getting Curtis out of the nappy first thing never occurred to Lawrencia; after all, to her mind, what did it matter? Kids were used to walking around squelching in their own shit. It was an opinion Jake did not share, and once he was properly awake he would make a point of removing the nappy from Curtis and wiping the kid's ass. He was mostly running dry now, and excessive use of a nappy would only set him back in his development.

The sound of the crashing metal on plastic was a result of Curtis playing his usual game of battles between two random toys. This time a large plastic Swiper the Fox was attacking, and apparently defeating, the smaller but metallic Decepticon, Ravage. Jake grinned, imagining a cartoon in which Dora the Explorer set Swiper up to be defeated by Ravage, anything to get the little fox from swiping her clues as she went on her little journeys.

Curtis noticed him looking, and jumped to his feet. 'Undle Jake!' he shrieked.

'Hey, champ,' Jake replied, trying to give his voice the same kind of excitement. But instead all that came out was a slur, his throat still dry and rusty from lack of use. Water was needed. Besides rehydrating the body, it helped lubricate the throat first thing in the morning, and on that point he had to give Amy props.

Before he could move, Curtis was on him. Immediately winded by the jumping kid, Jake could only lay back and take the punishment. He tried to not laugh, once his breath was back, but failed miserably. Although Curtis was pushing down on his already full bladder, seeing the mischievous glint in his brown eyes made Jake laugh. It was a look that reminded him of Will when they were kids, long before Will had become a serious adult and the concept of daring-do had been vanquished by an over dependent family.

Jake reached up to stop Curtis, before his bladder exploded, and sat up, the added weight of Curtis doing wonders for Jake's abdominals.

'Love you, champ, but Uncle Jake needs a pee.'

'I go toilet, too,' Curtis said, once he was placed back on the floor.

Jake stood up, not bothering to pick up the duvet that had fallen into a heap on the floor, having been dragged off him by Curtis' feet. 'Reckon you've been toilet enough for one morning.'

Curtis was no longer looking up at Jake, rather his eyesight was now lower. Jake glanced down to see what was so interesting. Damn. Morning glory was something so normal for him that he hadn't even considered the tangible evidence that would be displayed before Curtis. The boy was now pointing, and reached out. Jake stepped back quickly, and reached down for the duvet.

'Not for you, little buddy.'

Wasn't his fault he'd woken up needing a piss – he was a guy, what could he do? He wrapped the duvet around himself, not much caring for walking into the hallway with his boner on display. Lawrencia was in the kitchen by the sound of it, her voice no longer raised, her tones now placating. He guessed she was on the phone to Jimmy again; not for the first time this weekend.

'I want x-boxers,' Curtis said.

'Tell you what, we'll take you shopping when Uncle Billy gets back, see if we can find you some x-boxers. You stay here, play with Swiper, and I'll have a shower. Then we'll sort you out, okay?'

Curtis nodded, and with an 'okay' returned to his toys. Jake smiled and left the lounge, noting the time as he did. It was only twenty after seven. So early, and on a Sunday, too! Still, Jake reasoned, the sun was shining and Will would be home later. He suspected a good day ahead.

*

Lawrencia looked up as she heard movement in the hallway, and saw Jake shuffling his way towards the stairs, duvet gathered about him. He glanced in, and nodded, before carrying on his way. Lawrencia went to mouth a 'good morning' but was dragged back to her phone conversation. If you could really call it that.

'Oi, you still there, bitch?'

Lawrencia groaned at Jimmy's use of the word. 'Yes,' she said quietly, not wanting Jake to hear, 'I'm still here.'

'Good. So what the fuck you going to do about this?'

'Billy's back today, then I'll be over.'

'You fucking better be! I ain't no mug, so don't go treating me like one.'

In her mind she could see him clenching his fists, ready to dish out her punishment for staying away.

'You shouldn't be there anyhow. That queer fucking brother of yours is trying to control you. Told you before, your family is full of freaks. I bet my boy is gonna turn into some fucking homo.'

Lawrencia felt her hands shaking, and forced herself to steady them. Even though Jimmy couldn't see her, she still felt the need to keep up the pretence that he didn't scare her. Not that he ever believed otherwise, of course; there was no doubt as to who held the power in their relationship.

'I'll be back tonight, I promise. I can't come sooner with Jake here.'

'That sack of shit? I'll fuck him up, too, if he gets in my way.' The line was quiet for a moment, but for the grinding of teeth. Lawrencia smiled, glad that Jimmy was attempting to control his anger. 'Listen, babe,' he continued, his voice now full of reason and calm. 'I need that money or Tripod Tim will have my balls. And you know he won't stop there.'

The implied threat was clear. She hadn't met Tripod Tim, but she had heard enough tales of the sick things he got up to in his spare time to know that Curtis would suffer as much as Jimmy if he didn't get his money. She rubbed a knee with her free hand.

'We'll get it. You know Billy has always come through for us.'

'Too fucking right, that poof knows what'll happen if he don't. Right, I'm going. You better be home by seven at the latest. And make sure you bring my boy back. Don't want him around no poof anymore, got it?'

Lawrencia swallowed hard. 'Y-yes,' she managed to get out a second before the line went dead.

She placed the phone on the side and stood there, her mind blank, as she attempted to gain some control of her emotions. She didn't want Curtis to come in and see her crying.

She jumped as the immersion heater kicked in and she glanced up to where she imagined Jake was showering. Another person who she did not wish to see her cry.

Billy had to come home soon. She had until seven to talk to him, and hopefully find a solution to her problems. It was only a matter of time before Jake worked out that things were not getting better, and soon enough he'd start poking his nose in, and then the fireworks would start.

As much as a small part of her would love to see him kick the living crap out of Jimmy, she knew that was not the solution. She had no idea what Billy could do, but she at least trusted him. He had always been reliable, and she needed her big brother more than anything right now.

*

Maia watched the news report on the small hotel TV. She wanted to cry, to feel something, but all she felt was detached. Not even angry.

The news report told about the body of a young man, estimated to be around seventeen years old, that had been found in Southchurch Gardens in the early hours of the morning. Little was known about how he had died, but according to their sources, he had been found with a wooden stake in his heart. The police refused to give any official comment.

Maia knew exactly what had happened. Lomax had unleashed Darrell just as planned. And why? Simply for a distraction. While Darrell was off confronting Frederick (she knew, deep down, that in reality it was more likely that Frederick had simply toyed with him), she and Lomax had gone to Lucy Road to witness the results of Frederick's trap.

They hadn't remained for long, but they saw enough. An upiór shayde ravenously engorging itself upon the blood left there, consuming much more than was usual. Lomax had been in awe, while Maia found herself horrified. Lomax knew more than he was saying, and he would only ever tell her what he wanted her to know, but she didn't need to know everything to understand that whatever Frederick had let loose, it was so much worse than a normal upiór.

Once satisfied, and knowing that Frederick was returning to the area, Maia and Lomax went in search of Darrell. Before they even found him, she knew her brother was dead. The transfusion of her blood had given her a link with him; not only would he register as a human-upiór hybrid to other upiór, but he was now fully traceable for Maia.

'Leave him,' Lomax had told her as she bent down to pick the body up. 'What? We can't just—'

'We can, and we will. Let him be found. It will throw much into disarray, not just for Frederick, but for the Three too. Now is not the time for them to be united. Change is coming, Maia, and they must remain on the backfoot.'

Maia didn't understand, not fully, but she knew she had no choice but to obey. And so now she sat in the hotel room, watching the news about her brother's body being found.

And she felt nothing. Nothing at all.

*

Jake emerged from the bathroom, mostly dressed but for his naked feet, with the damp towel still around his neck. He went to enter Curtis' room to get his socks, but stopped, his eyes lingering on the foot of the staircase leading to the third floor.

He glanced to the other flight of stairs, and perked up his ears. It sounded like Lawrencia was in the lounge watching some talk show or other; they were never really his kind of thing, although Amy seemed to like them, too, and usually watched them on the +1 channels, but to him they all seemed much of a muchness. No real difference between them; full of sad bastards who liked to air their dirty laundry to the nation, and then got pissed off when people in the audience offered their own views on their 'private' lives. That Lawrencia was now watching one of those shows meant that Curtis was probably still sitting around in his shit-filled nappy, mostly being ignored.

He would see to Curtis once he went downstairs, but first he needed to do something. And so he ascended to Will's room.

Lawrencia had commandeered it last night, which had left Jake the sofa. Stepping into Will's room felt odd; like he was entering somewhere forbidden, despite having slept there only one night ago. There was a sense of lifelessness about the place, as if something integral to the ambiance of the room was missing. It looked much as it should, although the women's clothing strewn across the unmade bed was a new touch. They were so absurdly out of place that for a moment Jake could do nothing but just look at them, his heart growing cold because someone had invaded a space that was usually just Will's. That the clothes belonged to Lawrencia meant nothing.

Will never had anything remotely feminine in his room ever. He hated the cliché of it all; that a gay man was expected to be automatically feminine the moment he came out. Even when he had first come out to his folks, as a kid, Will took great offence at the way they had over-compensated by buying him 'girly stuff'. None of it had found its way into his room; most of it ended up in the bin. Sometimes Jake thought that was where the rift between Will and his parents really began. His mother's affair with Eon Adomako was just an afterthought in terms of the estrangement, as far as Jake could tell.

He started at the sudden vibration in his pocket, and reached for his phone. His heart beat faster in anticipation, certain that it would be Will finally calling to tell him what time he'd be home.

But before he hit the green key, he noticed Amy's name and his excitement abated.

'Hi,' he said.

'Hi? Oh, don't sound too excited.'

'Sorry,' Jake said, and he was. Usually his skin tingled just to speak to Amy. 'How you doing?'

'I'm good. You?'

Jake didn't answer for a second, and before he could find a good excuse for his reticence, Amy provided him with one.

'Not loving it with Lawrencia? Don't worry, hun, soon Will will be home and then you can come and see me. I'll make you your favourite dish, and we can curl up on the couch.'

That did sound great, but all Jake wanted was Will to come home, or at least to make contact. He closed his eyes, feeling like he was betraying Amy somehow, and in his mind's eye he could see Amy smiling at him, telling him that things would be fine. Will would be home, and everything would be as it was.

He felt dumb, the anxiety a part of someone else's emotional make-up, not his, but in the best part of thirty years he and Will had never really been apart. He wondered if this was how it felt to lose a limb...

*

Most of the day Eryn, along with Theodor and Celeste, had been in audience, meeting with various Essex based upiór. Some were the little people, the equivalent of bums, but they also got to talk with those who worked in positions of authority. Much like humanity, upiór were everywhere; government officials, company executives, others working in shops, some even sweeping streets and emptying bins. Their greatest asset was their invisibility. The obvious signs of vampirism were long gone, no more pale and ice cold skin, no fangs and aversion to sunlight, and thankfully no more hairy feet; as such the modern vampire didn't need to hide to protect themselves. Now they lived in plain sight, looking no different than the average Joe, albeit the average Joe who looked incredibly healthy due to the preternatural blood that sustained their bodies. But meeting these upiór was tiring, and sometimes boring, work.

Before the next batch, Eryn demanded a break, and it was something both Celeste and Theodor readily agreed to. Theodor went for a wander around Canvey Island, while Celeste went to see Frederick who was at his Chalkwell apartment doing more fruitless research through his copy of the Book. Both went with an entourage of bodyguards, a necessary precaution given the Sekhites awareness of the Three's current occupation of the Residence.

Eryn retired to her own private room in the Residence to put her feet up and watch the local news feeds. Although she could have done with some fresh air, she loathed the idea of walking around with bodyguards, since she knew she was under no personal threat, and so chose to remain in the Residence. Of all the mind-numbing activities she engaged in, watching the news was her favourite. She had lived a long time and seen so much, and none of it had served to improve her temperament, but instant news reports courtesy of television was probably her most favoured invention of the twentieth century, which only improved as the twenty-first century came on them. It was a good way to see how lame the human world was, and how trivial, but at the same time it only confirmed how bored of life she was.

Eryn had never asked to be an upiór, it was the only way Theodor could save her from Edward Lomax, although over time she had adapted to the unwanted life Theodor had given her. She was certainly not suited for it, but it was those qualities that got her a place in the Three. Her practiced cynicism brought a nice balance to Celeste's optimism and Theodor's quiet ruminations.

It was a rare thing when a news report caught her interest, and it seemed that Sunday was going to prove to be a rare day indeed.

The anchor woman was, with a misplaced smile, talking about the death of a sixteen-year old boy in Southchurch Hall Gardens, killed in what she called a 'vampire style slaying' in the early hours of the morning. She went on to talk about how an old woman, a resident of the nearby Kursaal council estate, was out walking her dog when she came across the dead boy, lying with a wooden stake in his heart.

The details of how he was found didn't bother Eryn so much as the fact that someone was killing people in the clichéd vampire way. Her hand unconsciously patted the red palm sized edition of the Sekhmet Codex that sat in her jacket pocket.

She had immediately placed the call to Rochelle Swanson. Eryn needed all the information she could get on the killing, especially the information not released to the public. In particular, the kid's name.

Once the call with Rochelle had ended, Eryn dialled a second number, one known only to her. She didn't think the Brotherhood would authorise such a killing, but she needed to check. Such unwanted attention at a time like this was bad news, and if the Brotherhood were involved...

Eryn had no problem in going directly to Julius if necessary.

*

Some hours later, after popping out to the North End Road market to grab a few bits, Jake was surprised to see Lawrencia's bag sitting at the bottom of the stairs when he walked through the front door. After placing the carrier bag on the kitchen side, he called out for her. She told him she'd be down in a mo, so he returned to the kitchen to wait. It was clear what was going on, and now he realised it was up to him to convince her to hang around a bit longer. Will had to be returning soon.

She entered the kitchen with Curtis, who she was holding with one arm. The little kid was fully dressed, complete with his corduroy jacket. Jake raised his eyebrows enquiringly, allowing her the opportunity to tell him what was happening.

'We're going home,' she said.

Curtis didn't seem to be too happy about this news, and he reached out for Jake. He stepped forward to take the boy, but Lawrencia pulled back out of his reach.

'What about your promise to Will?' Jake asked.

'Take a look around, Jake, do you see him? He's supposed to be back now, but where is he?'

'Lawrencia, anything could have happened. Train delays. You know how it is, Network Rail often do line work on Sundays.'

'Right, and that would add, what, almost a whole day to his journey? I don't think so.'

Jake had to admit she had a point. Will had work tomorrow, so for him to come back so late made no sense. 'Maybe he's just decided to stay on a bit longer?'

'Sure, and hasn't bothered to tell anyone at all?' It was clear from Lawrencia's expression what she thought of that idea. 'I thought things were going to change, that for once he'd actually help me. But he's screwed me over.' She turned away at the knock on the front door.

Jake glanced over, and through the narrow pain of glass he made out a shape that could only be Jimmy. No one else could still appear to be scum by their blurred outline.

'We have to go,' Lawrencia said, already moving.

Jake followed her to the door. 'You're something else, Lawrencia, Will has done nothing but help you since you came back from Manchester.'

She reached for the door, and looked back. 'Fuck the money, Jake. Do you really think that's all there is to me? I mean all this! You think I want to be stuck in this shit every day?'

Lawrencia's eyes darted to the door, and then Jake saw it. For the first time since she returned home, the truth was staring him in the face.

'Then don't go,' he said, reaching out for her. 'You and Curtis stay here; Jimmy won't kick off with me here.'

Lawrencia swallowed hard. 'You don't understand, Jake, no one does. I *have* to go.' Jimmy thumped on the door and Lawrencia jumped. 'Now,' she added, placing Curtis on the floor, opening the door.

As soon as he saw his dad, Curtis ran into Jake's legs and grabbed on for dear life.

Jimmy didn't appear to notice. All he saw was Lawrencia.

'What the fuck kept you? Told you that queer bastard wouldn't help.'

Lawrencia placed a calming hand on Jimmy's chest. 'Don't start. Let's just get home. Curtis needs his bed.'

As Lawrencia went back to get her bag, Jimmy spotted his son clinging onto Jake. 'What the fuck is this shit?' he asked. 'Curtis, get your arse outside right now!'

The boy only held on tighter. Jake felt his body tense. 'Don't talk to the boy like that, James.'

Naturally, Mr Bravado failed to notice the dangerous edge to Jake's voice. 'I'll do what I fucking like. When you get your own kids, then you can try and lecture me, bra. Now get your fucking arse out here, Curtis!'

Before he realised he was even going to do it, Jake carefully released himself from Curtis and launched himself at Jimmy.

'I said don't talk to the kid like that,' he said, his hand tightening around Jimmy's throat, slamming the man against the open door.

Behind him Lawrencia let out a breath of air. 'Jake, don't...'

'Why not? Look at him, Lawrencia,' he said, his eyes never leaving Jimmy, lapping up the fear in the idiot's usually vacant eyes. 'He's a piece of shit. Do you really need this scum in your life?'

'I...' Jake looked back at Lawrencia, and was struck by the panic written all over her ebony features. 'Please,' she said, the emotion raw, 'don't do this.'

Curtis was watching the scenario unfold, terror in his every tick. Seeing this, the fight went out of Jake as he realised Jimmy had led him to act in an even more horrifying way in Curtis' eyes.

With a curl of his lips, he released Jimmy and stepped back. Jimmy grabbed for his own throat, and rubbed it sorely.

Jake turned away. 'Fuck you all,' he said.

When he reached the kitchen he turned back, in time to see Jimmy about to close the door.

'Oi, *bra*,' Jake called.

The man had the sense to pause, his body tense, before he glanced back.

'Just one hair needs to be touched on that boy and you better believe I'll be coming for you.'

Jimmy clearly wanted to big himself up, but his own sense of self-preservation kicked in at the last second and he walked out of the house, closing the door behind him.

*

'Everything about this is wrong,' Celeste said.

Frederick stood at the small window in the slanted ceiling. He looked out over Chalkwell. 'I know. But I don't know why.'

'Do you still think he is the Seeker?'

Frederick wanted to say yes, but he could not lie to Celeste. He turned from the window and crossed the width of the living room, to sit crossed legged on the floor before Celeste. He looked up at her.

'I think... The ka, the soul of an upiór, is in him. I felt it nine years ago, and I felt it again when I met him on the train. But his hunger... The way his shayde acted?'

Celeste thought a moment, her expression serene, giving nothing away. She leaned forward. 'There is a reason we set up the Rebirth Council. New upiór are selected with great care. Only haemomaniacs give in to their blood lust and create upiór without the blessing of the Council.'

'I know,' Frederick said, lowering his head. 'But Will did not respond to the test as expected, he did not act in a way the Book prepared us for. And I...'

'You were blinded by your rage.'

'I was. And, as it turns out, with reason. The Brotherhood was involved in the test...'

'Yes, that is a mystery. But one I feel sure Eryn will get to the bottom of.'

'Eryn?'

'Of course. She is many things, *mon toujours*, among them tenacious. She'll get the answers we need.'

Frederick knew he should tell her then and there about Eryn, what he had seen in the Sekhite's mind, but he could not. Eryn was up to something, and Frederick wanted to know what it was. He needed proof before he exposed her, and although Celeste may well take him at his word, what he had seen was not proof. Tangible evidence was required.

'But what about Willem?' Celeste asked, returning the conversation full circle. 'Regardless of how and why he was given the First Death, he is now in pontus, and undergoing it in a way that we have never quite seen before. I have thought to contact Ai Ling, perhaps she is aware of something we are not.'

'No!' Frederick snapped, and immediately regretted it. 'Sorry, but, Celeste, that wouldn't be wise.'

'Why not? She is the head of the Council, she knows more about the Rebirth than anybody. Maybe she has seen something that will explain this, something most of us laypeople do not know.'

'Yes, that is possible. But we should let this play out, see where it takes us. Will shall soon be upiór, and if nothing else, we can then discover the answers to who and what he is. The origin of his ka.'

Celeste sat back again. 'I do not like this, Frederick. This goes against everything, and it is not a decision I should make alone. I will confer with Theodor and Eryn, but in the meantime, keep an eye on the shayde. It will manifest again tonight, and by tomorrow the Three will have made a decision regarding Ai Ling.'

It was the best he could hope for. But still Frederick did not like it. Whatever was going on with Will was his problem, and he felt that he should be the one to deal with it.

15. Out of the Shayde

Amy entered the living room, and handed Jake the cup of Bird of Paradise tea she'd promised him. He looked up, and she was touched by the gratefulness in his hazel eyes. She sat beside him.

'You okay, babe?' It was a bit of a rhetorical question really, since it was clear he was not okay. He had yet to tell her what it was, but since he'd arrived at her flat twenty minutes ago, wet from the rain that had kicked in while he was en route, he'd not said a lot. When he'd called, saying he'd be over, she was surprised since she expected him to stay at his mate's and wait until Will had got home.

She was glad he wanted to come over. She'd not really seen much of him since Friday. They had planned on her stopping at Will's last night, but Lawrencia refused to give up the bed and there was no way Amy was going to sleep on someone's couch, and it didn't matter how comfortable the Como sofa looked.

Jacob took a sip of the tea, released a breath of satisfaction and placed the cup on the occasional table. He sat back, and Amy snuggled up to him, placing her head on his chest so she could hear the gentle beat of his heart.

'Come on, tell me about it.'

He looked down at her and she smiled at him, but he didn't smile back. 'I think I've misjudged Lawrencia's situation.'

'You think she wants to be with Jimmy now?'

Jake shook his head. 'No, definitely not. But the abuse is way more than emotional. When he shouted at Curtis... She was physically scared. And Curtis. Can kids his age know real horror?'

Amy swallowed, and answered quietly, 'Yes, they can. Kids are more receptive to emotions than any adult. They've yet to build their filters, and so get the full spectrum of emotion. Not only theirs, but those around them.'

'You say that with remarkable certainty. Don't tell me you've studied psychology as well as everything else?'

Amy laughed lightly, grimly. 'No, experience.'

'Oh.'

'If Lawrencia is trapped, it's going to take a lot to get her out of it. But the longer she's there, the harder it'll get.' Amy paused. It wasn't something she liked to talk about, but if it helped Jake... 'My mum was almost destroyed by the time she got free.'

Jake squeezed her gently and kissed the top of her head. 'I'm sorry, I had no idea.'

'No reason you would. Don't worry,' she said, looking up again. 'I'm a tough cookie, I got over it. And I wasn't alone.'

'Ex-boyfriend?'

Amy chuckled. 'God no. My twin.'

'Twin?' Jake said, a suggestive tone to his voice.

'Yes, a twin. I doubt that Terrance would really be your cup of tea, though.'

'Ah, a guy. No, definitely no tickling of my fancy there.'

She gently slapped his belly. 'You nut. Anyway, back to my point. If something isn't done soon, the mental scars for Curtis will last a long time.'

Jake sighed. 'Will really needs to get back. I can't do anything for Curtis without him here.'

'I'm getting that.' Amy lifted her head to kiss Jake. 'He'll be back soon, then you'll sort this mess out.'

Jake looked away, his eyes drifting to the window and the storm that was building up outside. 'I hope so.'

*

Marine Parade, running the length of the main seafront, was known for its boy racers. Youths in their late-teens or early-twenties, cruising along the seafront in their cheap cars, pimped up with spoilers, fins, neons, and various other accessories added on to make the cars appear cooler than they actually were. They could often be heard long before they were seen, thanks to their over-powered speakers secreted in the boots or under the rear seats, almost always pumping out some techno beat distorted by the bass. It was more sound than music. Nine o'clock on a Sunday night was a prime time for them, blocking up the traffic along the seafront, sitting in their cars like they ruled the world, when in truth they were little more than an annoyance for those who liked a quiet stroll along the beach, or those who wished for a social drink outside the many pubs. The sound of music pumping from the arcades was one thing, it was a standard sound expected in a seaside resort, but the cacophony of the boy racers was not.

That Sunday was different, however; barely a car travelled the length of the seafront, the brilliant sun of the day dragging most away to garden barbecues and other events more interesting than simply driving up and down the seafront flashing off the latest addition to their economy cars.

Naturally, though, the quiet was never destined to last and it was simply a matter of time before someone decided to take advantage of the relative silence. Two such boy racers had chosen that night to race through Southend, from Leigh to Shoeburyness, each taking a different route to see who'd reach their destination quickest. Despite the moniker, boy races rarely actually raced, but on this occasion the title applied itself in a very literal way.

One chose to make the journey down London Road, eventually cutting down the backstreets and coming out on Pier Hill, which brought him nicely onto Marine Parade and the final stretch along the seafront to Shoeburyness. Unfortunately, such was his speed, and the adrenalin coursing through his body, that he wasn't really paying attention at the mini roundabout situated at the bottom of Pier Hill, and singularly failed to notice his buddy, who had chosen the backstreets through Chalkwell and Westcliff, shooting up the Western Esplanade and also onto Marine Parade.

The two cars collided in a mangle of metal and noise. The crash brought people out in their droves; from the pubs, the arcades, the shops, even across the road people emerged from Adventure Island to discover the source of the commotion.

Frederick was also drawn to the site of the accident, although not by the sound, but rather by the intense smell of blood. He had been up on

Lucy Road, awaiting the second stage of Will's Rebirth when he got a whiff of the scent. It was so strong that it could only come from a major accident, and he knew without doubt that it would be the place at which Will would manifest. No amount of blood packs could compete with the aroma of freshly spilled blood.

By the time Frederick arrived, the area of the accident had been cordoned off, access only allowed to emergency services. He had no problem with that, his eyesight wasn't so bad that he needed a ringside seat like most of the onlookers, whose own nosiness was helped by the spotlights put in place by the fire department to assist them in extracting the victims of the accident.

Frederick took to the bridge that led to the entrance of the Southend Pier, and looked down at the disaster below.

Two body bags lay on the road beside the accident, containing the two less fortunate occupants of the car that had come up the Western Esplanade. One had found himself smashing through the windshield, a result of thinking the seatbelt law did not apply to him, and the other had died when the driver's side was slammed and crushed into the bollard in the centre of the mini roundabout.

The pimped up orange Ford Escort still remained, one side looking like crumpled tinfoil, lifted almost off its side, half on and half off the roundabout. The passenger of the second car was a bit more fortunate, wearing his seatbelt as he did. He was now sitting in the back of an ambulance, his wounds being tended to, the paramedics ascertaining the severity of his broken arm. The car, a silver Fiat Punto, was wrapped around a lamppost at the bottom of Pier Hill, the driver still contained within, crushed against the dashboard and the door which had collapsed into his side when the Punto had spun on its axis and slammed into the lamppost. Firemen had their cutting equipment out, and were searching for the safest way to cut the young man out of the car, while paramedics sought to stabilise him during the delicate operation.

Frederick was entranced, not by the accident, but by the impossible thing he was seeing. As previously noted, upiór had an ability to see beyond the perception of humanity, and one such thing was the pontus. That it happened beyond human awareness was, to Frederick's mind, a convenience of evolution, a supernatural protection against those who would seek to destroy upiór in such a weakened and unaware state.

He had seen many fledglings go through it and knew the three stages well enough. Seventy-two hours, and three stages; stage one being the shayde, a shadowy essence of the person, driven by an unconscious need for blood, supping on the source of life which was then used to create a new protective shell and body for itself. This was stage two, an amorphous mass of skin. Pure flesh, covered in minute orifices that sucked up blood wherever it went, slowly feeding the developing body within the sack of skin. Finally, stage three; protected by the bubble of flesh, the upiór within feasted on blood for several hours before it broke free to begin its immortal life.

Will should have been on stage two, but as he watched, Frederick could see that was far from how it was.

The amorphous shape was, unbeknown to the humans watching, sitting astride the black body bags, draining the blood from the dead bodies within. Sitting astride was the only phrase Frederick could think of, since the body of Will was very clearly defined by the folds of flesh on the amorphous mass, which seemed to tighten more with every second that passed, clinging ever tighter to the body inside.

Frederick knew this to be stage three.

Once it had finished gorging itself on the dead bodies, the mound of flesh slid off the black bags and began to roll towards the Fiat Punto, where the firemen were now cutting the driver free.

Draining the dead bodies was one thing, the measurable evidence hidden from immediate discovery, but to drain a body in front of people was a risk Frederick could not allow. As busy as they were, it wouldn't be long before the paramedics noticed the blood disappearing from the crashed car, and the driver himself.

He had to act fast, draw the sack of flesh away from the devastation. Very few people stood on the bridge, most drawn to the better view afforded them by the cordon, but still he pulled back to the opposite side of the bridge and extended a single talon, with which he slit the skin of his right palm and shook the blood from the cut, letting the scent of preternatural blood catch on the breeze. The shapeless mass stopped, and for a moment seemed uncertain on its course, before turning slowly towards where Frederick was casting droplets of blood into the air.

Normal human blood was indeed a feast for an upiór in stage three, but there was no blood as intoxicating as that of another upiór. Just one reason why Red Source was so popular among the Initiates.

Now he had the attention of the thing that was to become Will the upiór, Frederick turned and began to jog away, certain that the mass of flesh would follow. A upiór's blood was a good draw in itself, but within his veins were traces of the blood of the Ancient, and such a source of richness was something the fledgling could never hope to resist.

*

To get to a more secluded spot he had to circumnavigate Pier Hill and cut his way up through the nature reserve known as Never Never Land, the only carry-over from the landowner's predilection for all things Peter Pan; once upon a time the amusement park was even named Peter Pan's Adventure Island, as if to punctuate the point. Once at the top of Pier Hill, Frederick cut around the Royals shopping mall and up the high street, all the while trailing the blood which served to keep the sack of flesh following.

It was fortunate that his blood was more appetising than human blood, since even at near ten o'clock there were many people on the High Street. Some walking towards the nightclubs and pubs for one last crazy night out before the humdrum of the working week began again, while families headed up the high street towards the bus station, after enjoying a day out at the seaside. These families invariably contained at least one child who had managed to graze their skin at some point during the day, but the minor wound was nothing compared to the lure of Ancient-enriched blood. Just as well, Frederick thought, somewhat amused by the notion of the youngsters screaming while some unknown force attached itself to their knees and began draining them of blood.

He carried on at a faster pace, before he was too tempted to find out.

Once he reached the top of the high street, he cut a right and emerged onto Chichester Road. People stood at the bus stops that lined the edge of the Victoria shopping centre. Frederick slowed down, not wishing to attract too much attention to himself. Once past the bus stops, he entered the multi-story car park that stood behind the Victoria, and started up the twisting ramp. He gathered his speed, and within minutes he was on the roof.

From his vantage point he could see out across to Southend Victoria train station and the many buildings beyond, including the Civic Centre and police station. To the left of them was the Queensway roundabout, with exits leading back into town, and away towards London Road and Leigh, and to the right was the residential area of Southend itself, including several nearby tower blocks, all standing taller than the car park. Frederick knew that anybody looking out of their windows would get a good view of what was about to happen, but all they'd really see was one man acting very oddly in the deserted car park. Not exactly an unknown occurrence for Southend. He was quite safe from any intervention of well-meaning, or possibly nosy, locals.

The squelching alerted him to the arrival of the mass of flesh, and as it emerged into the floodlights he saw that it was looking even less like a mound of flesh and more like a man trapped inside a large skin-coloured plastic bag. The trapped analogy worked even more when he saw how the being within was trying to force his way out, but clearly didn't quite have the strength needed and, like a chick needing the assist of its mother to break the shell of its egg, it was clear that Will needed a little more blood to give him the strength to break free.

Frederick lifted his torn hand high and, as a matador with his red cloak, he swished his hand around, the flying blood enticing the fledgling to attack.

Before he had a chance to consider the foolishness of his plan, Frederick found himself beneath the sack of flesh and felt a sense of being pulled away.

He closed his eyes, giving in to the sensation, and his mind drifted back to the small Prussian province of Posen, where, in 1722 he was a young man of little means. He lived with his ailing mother, dreaming of becoming a member of the Order of the Black Eagle and serving the 'Soldier King'. Such dreams were not to come about, however, since only days after his twenty-first birthday he met a visiting French woman, Gabrielle Maupassant. She was in Prussia selling works of art, while at the same time painting a portrait of King Frederick Willem. In short order, Gabrielle became enamoured with the young Frederick Holtzrichter, and he found himself subject to her seduction. A very willing subject at that, since he had never encountered a woman of such beauty before. She smuggled him into her chamber at the royal palace, and it was there that he lost both his virginity and his mortal life. It was also there that he discovered her true name; Celeste.

In his mind's eye he could see himself lying on her bed, having already been spent once. He looked down at his nakedness, watching the steady rise and fall of Celeste's head as she worked her mouth around his manhood. A sharp sting and he let out a gasp of ecstasy; it was as if a small sharp object had pierced his pleasure. He had never felt anything like it. His heartbeat fastened, the blood rushing to his hardness as it pulsated in her mouth...

His life ended there, being pulled down into Celeste, just as he was now being pulled up and out of his body by Will.

Once again his life was about to end; not the short mortal span he had endured for twenty-one years back in Posen, but the immortal life he had lived ever since.

Will's thirst was killing him, in the same way that he had killed Will two nights previously...

Panic gripped him; he could not die, he had a mission to complete. His role was too important!

With all the preternatural strength at his disposal, Frederick extricated himself from the mass of flesh and cast it aside. He stood slowly, taking deep breaths, having never felt so weak. His clothes were ruined. Blood and puss covered his trousers and shoes, and his linen top was a mess of greens and reds, barely a hint of the white beneath. For once he was glad he'd left his leather jacket at home.

He looked over at the source of his mucky clothing.

Now looking like a deflated balloon, the bag of flesh, torn and gashed open, spewing out more puss and excess blood, lay at the far end of the car park where Frederick had thrown it. He stepped closer, applying saliva to his hand wound, sealing it.

He stopped a few feet away, and watched as fingers ripped through the drying flesh. He waited until Will worked his way free.

Finally, he stood there, the man Frederick wanted, in all his naked glory, unseen by anyone but another upiór. For a while longer Will would continue to exist beyond the perception of humanity, while his new body acclimatised to the world he had entered.

Frederick stood there in silence, taking in the sight before him. Despite the blood and puss that covered his body, Will was exactly as Frederick remembered him from when he had stood in Frederick's bedroom, naked but for his boxer briefs, while he got changed into his suit for a night out at Zinc. Only this time there was no underwear to hide away the genitalia which now hung freely between his legs. Frederick smiled, certain that they were a bit more well-proportioned than had been hinted at in his bedroom. It was a fact that an upiór's first preternatural body was a copy of the original mortal body, only with all perceived imperfections removed. In Will's case, it appeared the only thing he considered imperfect was between his legs, but his unconscious mind had taken care of that while his new body had grown in the sack of flesh.

Frederick smiled. Typical human vanity.

But, Frederick noticed, something was still wrong. For there, left of his groin, was a scar. That just never happened, a new upiór body was perfect. No blemishes, no scars. And yet here one remained. And it was an unusual scar, in so much that it seemed to have a definite shape. If he didn't know better, Frederick would have even said it was a symbol, and it looked vaguely familiar.

Will did not notice the attention. He was looking around wildly, his eyes unable to fix on any one thing. He looked up at the night sky and, as if in response to his confusion, the heavens opened up and the rain came crashing down. He closed his eyes, clearly enjoying the sensation of the water hitting his face. The downpour served to remove all the ick from his naked body and, once cleaned, he reopened his eyes and looked directly at Frederick.

'Will,' Frederick said, with a smile, and took a single step forward, before stopping again. His smile dropped, once he noticed Will's translucent eyes. That was wrong as well. Upiór had transparent eyes, the blood clearly flowing behind them, but only near the Second Death after the pigment had drained away after hundreds of years.

'You,' Will said, his voice dry from lack of use. 'You did this to me.' He looked down at his nakedness, and when he looked back up Frederick was stung by the hatred directed at him. 'What did you do?'

'A favour. You were dying, I had to...'

'No.' Will shook his head. 'I... I cannot know this. It's too...' He grabbed his head and let out an almighty scream.

Frederick looked to his left. Several lights in the block of flats came on, the residents alerted by the piercing sound. Although not part of the tangible world yet, somehow the despair in Will's soul managed to tear through.

'It's too much,' Will was saying, 'too much. I will *not* know this. Not now.'

'What?' Frederick drew in closer, reaching out for Will, but with a force that surprised Fredrick, Will flung him aside.

Frederick crashed into the wall of the car park, and for a moment he remained there. His body crushed by the impact.

He was still much too weak from allowing Will to feast on him. His mind was awash with confusion, not able to make sense of what was happening. So much about the Rebirth was wrong. Frederick looked up, but Will was gone. Not able to stand, he reached out with his mind; now Will was out of the pontus the psychic connection should have been easy to establish.

But there was nothing.

No trace of Will at all.

*

He ran through the rain, barely noticing the water as it splashed down over his naked body. He didn't know where he was going, and he didn't care. He just had to run away from what he knew, what he didn't want to know. His head was a maelstrom of thoughts.

Memories; faces of all the people he had known over his very long life, places he had been, things he had done. Terrible, terrible things. The memories brought with them intense feelings of love, respect, anger, hurt, hate and, strongest of all, pity. Centuries of feeling pity for those who touched his life, unwilling to challenge the status quo of their lives, never willing to stand up and say 'no!'.

None knew true freedom but he. Freedom that was brutally stolen from him.

No!

He could not know any of this. And so, he would not. He would close it all away.

No one knew themselves as well as he did, no other could hope to understand their own minds as he understood his, and none had the control he did. Every little piece of himself, his history, everything that made him who he was. All of it would be sealed in a labyrinth of corridors, every memory slammed shut behind a door.

Even his name would be vanquished.

*

'What do you mean he's not back?'

Jake had put off the call as long as he could, but it was now ten thirty and still not a word from Will. There were a few people he wanted to call, but Amy had sworn him against doing so. 'No need to worry people needlessly. Maybe he missed his train, and will be back tomorrow.' Jake liked the thought of that, but nothing could excuse Will not even bothering to call.

'Just what I said, Steve. He should have been back hours ago. Have you heard from him at all?'

'Of course not, why would I—?'

'Because you're running his business while he's away.'

'Well, yeah, obviously there's that, I just meant...' Steve stopped talking abruptly, as if he'd only just realised he was making no sense. 'But no, not heard from him since Friday. I mean, he should be back for tomorrow as we've got to decide what to do with Kurt then.'

Will had told Jake all about that. It was one of many reasons he should have been back.

'Maybe he lost his phone?'

Another excuse Amy had come up with. 'I don't think so, Steve, and even if he had, he'd surely find a way to contact somebody.'

'You, um, don't think something has happened to him?'

Jake did think that, but... 'I've been checking the net, watching the news. Only thing that I can find that has happened in Southend this weekend is some kid getting killed, and a big crash.'

'You sure he wasn't... I mean, I dread to think he was, but...'

'No. I contacted the police in Southend. They won't give out names yet, but they assured me that none of the casualties were Will.'

'That's a relief.'

Jake didn't think Steve sounded relieved. 'Okay, well, just thought I'd check. Hopefully he'll turn up tomorrow.'

'Yeah. Hopefully. Keep me informed, yeah?'

Jake said he would, and Steve hung up before Jake could even say goodbye. He tried not to think it, but Steve sounded a little skittish, like he was on something. Maybe he was. Will often told him how Steve was an adrenaline junkie, maybe that wasn't the only kind of junkie he was. Wouldn't be the first person to be like that in Will's life.

Jake stood up and walked over to the bay windows. He decided he would stay at Will's one more night at least, just in case Will turned up really late.

The house was so quiet.

'Will, where the fuck are you, man?'

Epilogue

There was a naked man in her garden.

Lizette Cranna liked to think she lived a simple life; a history lecturer at the University of Southend, she lived on her own, the cliché mad cat woman. Of course, she wasn't mad, but she did have cats. Many of them. And even more visited regularly. Her home life was simple; outside of the usual chores, she tended to spend a lot of her time reading books (academic, historical stuff as a rule – she made exceptions for authors like Tom Holland), watching documentaries (she wasn't really one for films) and, occasionally, she would be dragged out for a bit of social interaction by her colleagues, in particular her TA, Jordan. Of course, all of this was dependent on *her days* with the kids. Most of the time her kids (both teenagers now) lived with their dad in Basildon, but they still visited regularly, and stopped over every other weekend.

This weekend, though, had been very much an indoor one. The weather had been appalling for a start, even for a March in Chalkwell. Gale winds, sheet rain, and last night even a bit of thunder. It was supposedly all going to change tomorrow, but Lizette had very little faith in weather forecasts. The only way to know for sure, was to open the curtains in the morning and hope.

Her evening, now drawing to a close, had seen her curled up on her sofa reading *Queens of the Wild*, a study of pagan goddesses in Christian Europe. She'd been so engrossed, in fact, that she'd lost track of the time. Which, she had to admit, was nothing new. It was only the appearance of Garth, her ginger tom, and his desire to sit on the book, that had pulled her out of the little world she was in.

She tapped her phone, and the screen lit up, revealing it to be 22:48, and thus almost half hour after her bedtime. With a sigh, and a yawn, she stood and immediately Garth was in her spot.

'Make sure you keep it warm for me,' she said, smiling.

She popped the book, face down and open, on the coffee table, and walked over to the bay window to close the curtains. Her slim shadow flickered on the rear wall, cast by the flames burning around the logs in the fireplace. It may not have been the safest way to warm a room, but she liked to think of herself as an old-fashioned girl and it was the cheapest and best option.

Despite the storm outside, the top window was open a crack, letting in the fresh air from the nearby Thames Estuary. Lizette paused before closing the curtains, and looked out, enjoying the way the wind cast the small tree at the far end of the garden from side to side, rustling the bushes that lined the...

She blinked.

She shook her head. She must have been mistaken. But she was sure she'd seen a shape leaning tightly against one of the wet bushes. A human shape.

She was often told about her recklessness, not least by Linden, the kids' dad, and she supposed that's what played into her decision to investigate. Of course, she knew she was being daft. Going out into the dark garden in such weather was stupid enough, but to confront a stranger in her garden...

She went to the kitchen and switched on the garden floodlights. They didn't illuminate the spot the person was in, but they helped a little.

The shape pushed itself even closer to the bush, now seeking cover from the light as well as the rain.

Well, she thought, *can't have that in my garden.*

Lizette popped on her mac and wellies, and stepped outside. 'Excuse me,' she said, her voice raised against the wind. 'Who are you?'

The person looked up and for a second Lizette was sure she saw a pair of red eyes looking at her. Probably a trick of the lights behind her.

'Step into the light, please,' she told the shape. 'This is private property, and I'd rather like to see who I'm talking to.'

Polite to a fault, that was her problem. Or so Jordan told her. That always amused, since she argued that it was difficult to sound *that* polite when you have a Scots brogue to your accent. But then, considering the way Linden used to walk over her...

The person continued to look at her, drawing her in.

'Well?' She wasn't willing to go any nearer.

And yet, she noticed, she had moved closer. She forced herself to stop.

The shape stood, took a step forward. Not far, but enough for the light to pick him up a little better.

And it was a him. A man. A *naked* man.

Lizette tried not to look closer, but what woman could ignore a naked man standing before them?

He was in good shape. The cold weather probably worked against him in certain areas, but that didn't spoil the sight, Lizette considered with a slight appreciative smirk. He was slim, but with definition in his muscles. He wasn't especially tall, could be no more than 5' 10, with dark hair and thin eyebrows. His eyes were narrow, and definitely had a strange redness to them which had nothing to do with the light.

He stepped closer to her, but she felt no sense of threat and so held her ground.

Don't be bloody stupid, you numpty, the voice inside her head said. But she ignored it. There was a naked man, a good looking, fit naked man in her garden and she...

Well. She was being stupid.

But look at him!

It had been a long time since she'd enjoyed the company of a handsome man. And an even longer time since she'd got naked with...

She shook her head. Dangerous thoughts.

'That's better,' she told the man, who had now stopped. He just stood there, the rain running down his naked body. 'Who are you?' she asked him. 'What's your name?'

The man frowned. 'I... don't know,' he said, stumbling over the words like he'd never used them before. 'Who am I?'

Well, Lizette thought, *that complicates things.*

To be continued in...
ORACLE